SP

KISS & KILL

Also in the **SPECIAL AGENTS** series:

SPECIAL AGENTS
KISS & KILL

sam hutton

With special thanks to Allan Frewin Jones

HarperCollins *Children's Books*

Disclaimer: This is a work of fiction. Any references to real people, living or dead; and real events, businesses, organisations, and localities are intended only to give the fiction a sense of reality and authenticity. All names, characters, places and incidents either are the product of the author's imagination or are used fictitiously, and their resemblance, if any, to real-life counterparts is entirely coincidental.

First published in Great Britain by HarperCollins *Children's Books* 2004
HarperCollins *Children's Books* is a division of HarperCollins*Publishers* Ltd
77-85 Fulham Palace Road, Hammersmith, London W6 8JB

The HarperCollins *Children's Books* website address is
www.harpercollinschildrensbooks.co.uk

3

ISBN-13 978   0 00 714845 5
ISBN-10   0 00 714845 3

Text and series concept © Working Partners Limited 2004
Chapter illustrations by Tim Stevens

Printed and bound in England by Clays Ltd, St Ives plc

Prologue

Northwest London.

August 14th.

23.53.

Her Majesty's Prison – Wormwood Scrubs.

A long, high brick wall. A gatehouse with two thick, angular towers. A white stone arch. Solid wooden gates, locked for the night.

Danny Bell stared out through the darkened windows of the Mobile Surveillance Unit. His small, powerful binoculars were concentrated on the gates. Sweat ran down his neck. His clothes were sticking to him.

It was a humid, sultry night. Silent. Ominous. Something was about to happen.

He wiped his sleeve over his face. The van was stiflingly hot, but they couldn't open a window. Someone might see them. That could wreck everything.

By the time Danny's eyes returned to the binoculars, the gates were open. His breath hissed. An ambulance came bolting out of the darkness. The siren began to wail. Blue lights flashed.

He spoke into the microphone of a lightweight headset.

"Michael Stone has just left the building. Operation Babysitter is go."

✪

Alex Cox sat in the back of the racing ambulance. The nineteen-year-old London-born PIC agent was poised and watchful. There were two prison guards with him, as well as a doctor.

Alex's attention was focused on the figure lying on the stretcher.

The patient was a heavy-set man in his fifties. His iron-grey hair was cropped close to his bullet skull. His bulldog face was pallid and greasy with sweat. A clear plastic mask fed him oxygen. The prison doctor hovered anxiously over him.

Two guards sat on the other side of the ambulance. One was a solid, grim-faced man in his forties, the other a much younger man. Late twenties, Alex guessed. New to the game, under stress, staring at Mickey Stone as if he couldn't quite believe he was sharing space with the man who had once run virtually all of London's criminal underworld.

The ambulance careered to the left and sped along Du Cane Road. Their destination was Hammersmith Hospital – no more than five minutes away.

Alex was alert to his fingertips – things could start happening at any moment. He had to be ready.

"Will he be OK?" the younger guard asked.

The doctor looked round. "We have to get Mr Stone to hospital as quickly as possible," he said. "A cardiac infarction can have serious consequences if it isn't treated immediately."

The older guard put his hand on the younger man's shoulder. "Don't waste your time worrying about him, Barry," he said. "Stone's got more lives than a cat."

Barry Dean had been the first to respond to the agonised shouts from Mickey Stone's cell. He had been the one who had found Stone writhing on the bed, clutching at his chest – his face grey and deathly. Barry had only been in the prison service for three months: he was still learning the ropes.

A voice spoke in Alex's earpiece.

7

"How's it going?" It was Danny from the MSU.

"Fine," Alex said tersely. "ETA at the hospital is twelve-o-five."

"And the patient?" Danny asked.

"He's a very sick man, Danny," Alex said expressionlessly.

"Poor guy. Don't you go losing him, Alex."

"I'll try not to."

There was a heave of activity from the bed. Mickey Stone reached out an arm and caught a fistful of the doctor's shirt. "The pain!" he groaned, his eyes bulging. He sat up, his voice grating slowly through his oxygen mask. "Do something... about... the pain!"

The older guard bent forwards and prised the doctor free. "You'll get something for the pain soon enough, Stone – you just behave yourself."

Stone winced and fell back. Alex watched him. If the man was faking it, he was putting on a great act.

"I'll give him a jab," the doctor said. "That should calm him." He crouched down and opened his medical box. Alex noticed that the doctor's hands were shaking as he took out a hypodermic needle and drew clear liquid into it from a small glass bottle.

❈

Danny sat at a bank of hi-tech electronic equipment in the back of the MSU. He ran his hands over dials and faders and touch-sensitive controls. His job was to channel information. Two Police Investigation Command cars were parked in Braybrook Street. Backup in case of problems. Each car held four armed agents. No one was taking any chances.

Back at HQ – at PIC Control – DCS Jack Cooper was listening intently to Danny's brief, precise transmissions. Tension was running high. Operation Babysitter was a gamble, but it was a gamble that Jack Cooper felt he had to take.

Mickey Stone had been on remand now for twelve months. Jack Cooper had coordinated the arrest of the Stonecor kingpin. It had been the culmination of many months of effort – and it had had terrible personal consequences for Cooper and his family. The date of Stone's trial was coming up fast. If convicted, he would be spending a very long time behind bars.

Stone wanted out. PIC knew he was going to make a bid for freedom. Operation Babysitter had been set up to ensure Stone's escape went according to plan: according to Jack Cooper's plan.

Danny spoke into his mike. "Alex says everything's fine," he said. "So far so good, huh?" Jack Cooper could hear the tightness in Danny's voice. The black American trainee was only eighteen years old, but

Cooper had great faith in him. Danny had designed the miniature tracer bugs that were attached to Stone's clothing. He had designed half the cutting-edge gear that filled the MSU. Danny was an electronics genius – that was why he was there.

"Keep alert," Cooper growled into the desk mike.

"You bet," came the breathless response. The channel went dead as Danny switched to update the waiting cars. Split-second timing was vital. Either the cogs of Operation Babysitter were going to mesh perfectly, or...

"Or" wasn't an option.

❂

The doctor withdrew the needle from Mickey Stone's arm. He glanced at the two guards. He was getting twitchy. The sweat running down his face wasn't just from the heat – he was close to panicking. Something was about to go down, Alex was convinced of it. He tensed his muscles, ready to react in an instant.

The grey colour left Stone's face within moments of the injection. Whatever the doctor had given him, it was powerful and fast acting. His cheeks became ruddy and his eyes, which had been bulging and rolling with agony, narrowed, glittering like broken glass.

The doctor reached down again into his medical box.

"Hey!" The older guard clearly suspected something. He leaned forwards. Stone sat bolt upright, his arm swinging across like a hammer, knocking the man sideways – stunning him for a moment.

Alex sprang forward. He came to a sudden halt, staring at a gun that the doctor had thrust into Mickey Stone's waiting hand. Stone pulled the oxygen mask off. He ripped the monitoring pads off his chest. The doctor backed away.

Mickey Stone stared at Alex. "Do you want to take me on, boy?" he said.

Alex lifted his hands, palms outwards. "You've got the gun, Mr Stone," he said. "No one needs to get hurt here."

The older guard was on the floor of the ambulance. He wiped a trace of blood off his lip. His eyes smouldered with anger.

"You stay right where you are," Stone told him. He looked at Barry Dean. "Hand me the intercom, lad," he said. Barry stared at him as if transfixed.

"Do it!" Stone bellowed.

Barry scrambled to get the hand-held intercom. Stone snatched it, his eyes constantly flickering from Alex to the older guard, the gun ready in his fist.

Mickey spoke into the intercom. "Louie? We're in

11

control back here," he said. "Make for the pick-up point – and step on it."

The final piece slotted into place. Alex had known that the doctor was in on the act – but he hadn't known until that moment that they were also being driven by one of Stone's accomplices.

The ambulance lurched forward with a sudden surge of speed.

Alex hoped that Danny was on the ball. This was the critical moment.

Stone's eyes were fixed on Alex with a look of ice-cold hatred. Alex stared back at him. Unafraid.

"Doc!" Stone barked. "Find something to tie the big boy up with." He nodded towards the older guard. The doctor bound the man's wrists and ankles with lengths of bandage.

Barry Dean was staring at the gun with wide-open eyes. He was shaking, his face a mask of fear. Alex glanced at him. He was concerned that the inexperienced guard might do something brave and dangerous. Something that might start the bullets flying. Alex wanted to prevent that at all costs.

"Hey, Barry," he called. "It's going to be fine. Just keep calm." He looked at Stone. "The wonders of modern medicine, eh, Mr Stone?" he said with dark humour. "Tell me, how did you fake the heart attack?"

Stone smiled grimly. "The doc gave me a little pill," he said. "A pill to bring it on – and an injection to take it away." His eyes hardened. "Except that the doc didn't tell me how much it was going to hurt." He frowned. "That wasn't part of the deal, Doc."

"There was no other way," the doctor mumbled.

"We'll discuss that later," Stone said. He looked at Alex. "Meanwhile, me and Mr Cox here have some things to talk about." He lifted the gun and aimed it at Alex's head. "I want some information from you, boy, and if I don't get it, I'll give you something to put you to sleep permanently."

✪

Danny had created a patch-through that allowed the people at Control to hear everything that was coming to him through Alex's lapel mike. He was also monitoring signals coming in on a separate device. Red dots on a series of constantly sweeping screens. Three tracker bugs.

One sewn into the collar of Stone's shirt. Another in the waistband of his trousers. The third hidden in his watch. Microchips. So long as Stone was within five miles of the satellite-boosted surveillance range of the MSU, they'd be able to follow his every movement.

13

Danny registered the sudden increase in speed of the ambulance on the MSU radar gun.

"They're taking off," he said into the mike. "56 kph, and rising fast." He spoke to the waiting cars. "OK. It's show time – we're hitting the road. You boys keep out of sight. We don't want any foul-ups."

Danny spoke to his own driver. The MSU was going to keep well back. The sight of the white PIC van might spook Stone, and a spooked Michael Stone was *not* something that they needed. Not with Alex and two guards in the ambulance with him, and not now that Danny knew for certain via Alex's mike that Stone was packing a gun.

The tracker bugs would do the job.

Danny clicked to Alex's channel. "We're right behind you, buddy," he said.

There was no response, but he hadn't expected one. Alex had other work on right now.

Danny leaned back and wiped the sweat off his forehead. He looked at the three monitor screens, feeling a sense of pride that it had been his own innovations that had helped make the tracker bugs so small they could be put into Stone's clothing without him suspecting a thing.

"Boy genius strikes again," he murmured to himself, smiling. "I should get some kind of award."

One of the red dots winked out.

Danny stared, not trusting his eyes for a moment. He jerked upright, his fingers moving over faders and dials. Nothing. The bug in Stone's collar had failed.

Damn!

The second of the red lights went out. Danny let out a moan of frustrated concern.

"What the hell..."

Danny worked frantically at the electronics bank. One failure was just about possible. Two were definitely suspicious.

"Alex?" Danny spoke into the mike. "Two of the bugs have gone down. I can't hear what's going on over there." It was then that the silence from Alex's mike hit home. Danny turned dials. He'd been so busy congratulating himself that he hadn't even noticed it had all gone deadly quiet from the ambulance.

Danny switched channels. "Boss?" he said.

"I'm here," came Cooper's deep growl. "I don't hear anything from the ambulance. What's happening?"

"We've got problems, Boss," Danny admitted. "Two bugs are down and I've lost contact with Alex." Even as he spoke, the last of the tracker-bug lights went off. The three screens swept round and round, monitoring nothing.

"The last one's just gone," Danny said. "Stone must have found them and smashed them. We don't have any way of tracking him once we lose him on visual. He'll vanish, Boss – I'm telling you: he'll be history!"

Operation Babysitter had gone seriously and catastrophically wrong.

Chapter One

Precisely 13 hours and 43 minutes earlier.

PIC Control, Centrepoint.

The Briefing Room.

The final run-through of Operation Babysitter.

In attendance: DCS Jack Cooper. His personal assistant, Tara Moon. Twenty-five years old – tall and lithe with short red hair and fierce green eyes. The three PIC trainees: Danny Bell, Alex Cox and Cooper's own sixteen-year-old daughter, Maddie.

There were several other agents in there as well – PIC operatives who needed a detailed understanding of the upcoming operation.

On each computer screen there was a picture of

Mickey Stone and a brief rundown of his life and crimes.

Maddie Cooper had good reason to be interested in Mickey Stone and his criminal empire.

One of Stone's associates had gunned down the Cooper family on a rainy London night just over twelve months ago. There was little doubt that Stone had ordered the assassination. It hadn't quite worked. Jack Cooper was in a wheelchair, but he had survived. Maddie's hopes of being a professional dancer had been destroyed, but she too had survived. Maddie's mother had not.

Maddie had a lot of reasons for hating Mickey Stone. But it was not hatred that drove her now, it was a desire to see justice done. She had grown up a lot over the past year: she had discovered a new way forward for herself – as a fast-track trainee in PIC.

The digitized picture of Stone disappeared off everyone's screen. It was replaced by a picture of a middle-aged man. Well dressed. Well groomed. Arrogant-looking.

"For those of you who don't know this gentleman," said Jack Cooper, "let me introduce you to Maurice Simms. Mr Simms has been Stonecor's legal representative for the past thirteen years. Stone trusts him completely." Cooper turned to Tara Moon. "Would you like to explain why he's wrong to do that?"

Tara nodded. "Simms has been a bad boy," she said, her face impassive. "He's been doing some business on the side with some very unpleasant guys from Colombia."

Maddie knew what that meant: hard drugs. Cocaine, or heroin. Evil stuff.

"We've been on Simms's tail," Tara continued. "We have enough evidence now to put him away for several years and – following a conversation we had with him a few weeks back – he knows that he's going down for a long stretch unless he helps us."

Alex frowned. "Have we done a deal so we drop the charges if he cooperates with us?" he asked.

"No," said Jack Cooper. "We've agreed to put in a good word for him at his trial. That's all."

"Simms has been visiting Stone regularly in Wormwood Scrubs," Tara said. "Which is how come we know Stone is planning to escape tonight."

"Tonight?" said Danny. "I thought we'd have a few more days. I haven't had time to test the bugs properly."

Alex glanced at him, half smiling. "I suppose we could ask Stone to wait for a few days," he said. "When should I tell him you'll be ready?"

Danny held his hands up. "OK. Point taken. I'll run the final tests today."

"We need the bugs up and running by two o'clock," Jack Cooper told him. "Simms is due to visit Stone this afternoon, and I want Alex at the prison at the same time. He can plant the bugs, and he can make final contact with Simms."

"By three o'clock this afternoon, we should know the details of the escape plan," said Tara. "That's when we put Operation Babysitter into action."

Maddie clicked her computer mouse and her screen changed to a high-security file she had put together on her father's instructions.

Operation Babysitter

Background Information:

Michael George "Mickey" Stone's trial will begin at the Old Bailey in three weeks' time. Stone has two very good reasons to wish to avoid the trial:

1. Stonecor's legitimate business operations hide a huge criminal empire. One of the men who helped run Stonecor is Richard Bryson. He is currently in custody. He has agreed to give evidence against Stone at the trial. He knows enough to do Stone a lot of damage.

Bryson has a lot of other information concerning Stonecor, which he is not prepared to hand over until Stone and his son, Eddie, are in prison. Bryson will then undergo extensive plastic surgery to alter his appearance, and he will be given a new identity and relocated. This has been agreed. Bryson is being protected in safe houses until he is needed at the trial.

2. Mr Stone is anxious to re-establish personal control over his criminal empire. Although Mr Stone still exerts great influence from his prison cell, rumours have been circulating through the criminal world that Eddie is still alive, and eager to take over where his father left off...

Maddie stared at that name on her screen. Eddie. Eddie Stone.

She had good reason to remember him.

It had been her first case. Danny, Alex and Maddie had been working together for the first time. They had been at a house in Holland Park, owned by Stonecor. Things had got out of hand. Badly. Eddie Stone had taken Maddie hostage. He had escaped with her in a helicopter. But Maddie hadn't gone quietly. She had fought him. A wild kick had wrecked the helicopter's controls over the River Thames. Eddie had taken a dive into the deep brown water – leaving Maddie at the controls of the doomed aircraft. Somehow she had managed to bring it down safely in the shallows. Eddie had vanished. At the time, he had been presumed dead: drowned in the murky river water. That was then. This is now...

Recent intelligence suggested that Eddie Stone was alive. Holed up abroad, making plans for a major comeback.

Maddie continued to read her file.

PIC has learned that a UK-wide criminal summit is going to be held in London very soon. We do not have the precise date of this meeting yet, nor a location. Sources lead us to believe that Eddie Stone is going to the summit to stake his claim as the new controller of Stonecor.

It is certain that Mickey Stone will do whatever he can to prevent this from happening.

PIC analysis of the situation:

Mickey Stone will attempt to escape from Wormwood Scrubs in the very near future in order both to avoid the

*trial and to reclaim his hold over the Stonecor empire.
He will go to the criminal summit to prevent his son
from usurping him.*

*If Mickey Stone is prevented from escaping, Eddie
Stone will take over Stonecor. If this happens, Richard
Bryson will not give us any more information and we
will be unable to close Stonecor down. Eddie Stone has
been living abroad for several months now, and there is
a good chance that, once he has control of Stonecor, he
will run the company from outside the UK.*

*Operation Babysitter will allow Mickey Stone to
"escape", whilst keeping him under permanent close
PIC surveillance. He will lead us to the criminal summit.
PIC forces will move in. Mickey Stone will be rearrested,
and Eddie Stone will also be taken into custody.*

❂

The same day. 14:00.

Shepherd's Bush, London W12.

A man and a woman were in a small room at the top of
a semi-derelict Victorian building. The heat of the summer's
day was intense. The room was airless and stifling.

The woman sat in an old armchair. The cover was
faded and ripped. Stuffing bled out in grimy chunks.

She was tired. Her name was Alice Chang. She was a PIC agent, twenty-seven years old, with eight years of police experience under her belt. Alice longed for her shift to be over. She was due to be relieved at three o'clock, and then she had to be back here at midnight for the graveyard shift.

Richard Bryson was on his hands and knees on the filthy, bare floorboards. He had his ear to the floor. Listening.

Alice Chang eyed him expressionlessly. She thought he was probably crazy. Guarding him was no picnic. She was one of a team of four, giving him 24/7 protection until he was needed at the Old Bailey.

The secrecy of the location was vital. Mickey Stone still had plenty of friends and helpers out there, and there would be a big reward for the man who silenced blabber-mouth Richard Bryson for all-time.

Bryson lifted his tousled head and stared at her. "I can hear them," he said. "There are rats down there. I can hear them scuttling about. This whole place is one big rats' nest. It should be condemned."

Alice Chang arched an eyebrow. "It has been," she said. "That's why you're here."

Bryson glared at her, baring his teeth. He scrambled to his feet. He looked bad. His clothes were crumpled, his hair uncombed. His face was stubbled and drawn.

His eyes flickered about – half mad. At any moment he expected the door to be kicked down. Assassins. It was only a matter of time.

He'd been living like this for sixteen weeks.

He stalked the room, corner to corner, his shoulders hunched, sweat running down his face. Alice Chang followed him with her eyes. He was a wreck.

He made a sudden lunge with his foot. A cockroach popped as he stamped on it. He turned on her. "I won't be treated like this," he shouted. He spread his arms. "I'm not putting up with this any more. I'm a star witness. I'm the man who's going to put Mickey Stone behind bars for the next twenty-five years. And I'm being kept in squalid holes like this. I expected four-star hotels. I deserve four-star hotels." He stared at her. "And what do I get?" He counted off on his fingers. "I get a filthy little room in Dalston. I get a flea-ridden bedsit in Streatham. And now I'm in this rat hole in Shepherd's Bush."

Alice Chang looked at him. "Can you keep it down, please?" she said. She wiped her hot forehead with a pocket handkerchief. "To be honest with you, Mr Bryson, I couldn't care less about your problems."

Richard Bryson moved angrily towards her. She sat up – her eyes steely, her muscles tensed for action. Bryson backed off.

25

"If it wasn't for me," he said sullenly, "you people wouldn't have anything on Mickey." He beat his chest. "I'm the poor sucker risking his neck by giving evidence against him." He gave her a hollow stare, his voice suddenly quiet and steady. "Do you have any idea what they would do to me if any of Mickey's people found out where I was?"

Alice Chang felt a twinge of compassion for him. He was obviously scared witless.

"They won't find you," she said. "That's the whole point of keeping you in places like this." She smiled, trying to reassure him. "Besides," she said. "Look on the bright side, we haven't had any of that music through the walls today."

As if on cue, a blast of tuneless rock music erupted from the house next door. Richard Bryson threw his hands over his ears and sank down on to his dishevelled single bed with a low moan.

Alice Chang looked at him. At least now he wouldn't be able to hear the rats.

She glanced at her watch. Fifty minutes and she'd be out of there.

Bryson cradled his head in his hands and began to rock back and forth in time to the hammering music.

Fifty minutes seemed like a long, long time to Alice.

Jack Cooper's office was on the top floor of Centrepoint in the heart of London. His wheelchair faced the broad windows. He was gazing out over a spectacular panorama of the city. Maddie was just behind him, sitting on the corner of his desk. She had brought him a sandwich.

Jack Cooper was taking a short break for lunch. It was rare for the two of them to share such personal time together. For Jack Cooper, work always came first. That was just the way things were, Maddie understood that. Her father had absolute authority and responsibility for the hand-picked agents of PIC. He answered only to the Home Secretary and the Prime Minister. He had to be one hundred per cent committed to hold down that job. Maddie was more proud of her father than she could ever put into words.

"You seem tired, Dad," she said gently. "How much sleep did you get last night?"

He glanced round at her. "The usual," he growled.

"Oh, right. Three hours." She frowned. "I'll set Gran on you if you don't start looking after yourself."

"Once this business is done with, I promise I'll sleep for a week," he said. "Deal?"

"Deal." She slid off the desk and stood by his side. "Are you worried?" she asked.

He looked up at her. "PIC is an expensive organisation, Maddie," he said in an oddly subdued voice. "I have to produce results. There are plenty of people out there who'd like to get their hands on our funding. Special Branch. Special Operations Executive. MI5..." He waved a hand towards the wide blue skyline. "Sometimes it feels like there are vultures circling this office, Maddie. Waiting for me to make a slip."

"So, Operation Babysitter needs to go smoothly," Maddie said.

Jack Cooper nodded.

"No problem," Maddie said with a smile. "With Danny, Alex and me on board, what could possibly go wrong?"

Her father laughed softly. He took her hand for a few moments.

"Once the Stones have been put away, Bryson will start to talk," he said. "And if he knows half as much as he's hinting at, his evidence will do so much damage to organised crime in this country that it'll take them twenty years to recover."

Chapter Two

Wormwood Scrubs.

The same day. Early afternoon.

The cell doors stood open all along the narrow grey corridor.

Alex's footsteps echoed. He walked briskly, feeling the claustrophobic effect of all those heavy steel doors and of all those locks and bars that shot home behind him.

An inmate scuttled along at his side. A small man with a clever, sharp-eyed face and thin, slicked back hair. He was known as Gabby the Flap. Alex had no idea what his real name was.

Gabby was leading Alex to the prison chapel.

Two men eyed Alex and Gabby as they walked. Cold-eyed. Unimpressed. Alex knew them both. Tommy-no-Tongue and Rat Boy Flynn. Bad characters.

Tommy smirked as Alex passed him. "Looks like they'll let anyone in this place these days," he said.

Alex paused and looked at him. Tommy held his eyes for a few moments then looked away. The smirk was gone. Tommy had been on the wrong side of Alex in the past – he knew better than to push him too far.

Alex carried on walking.

More keys turned in locks. More doors opened and closed.

Two big men stood in the entrance to the chapel. Alex knew them both. Sledgeman, an all-in wrestling pro and part-time burglar. Tapper John, big as a haystack and solid muscle from his shaven head to his feet. They were Stone's bodyguards. They towered over Alex, blocking his way.

"Mr Stone is busy right now," said Tapper John.

"He'll make time for me," Alex said. He pushed against Tapper John. A fist the size of a ham came ramming out, catching a hunk of Alex's shirt and pushing him backwards against the wall.

"Mr Stone is busy right now," Tapper repeated.

Alex took hold of Tapper's huge fist and slowly

prised the fingers open. Tapper seemed surprised by this show of strength.

Alex looked into his eyes. "Muscle isn't everything," he said. "Skill is what counts." His arm shot up and his hand gripped Tapper John's neck. "Right between my index finger and my thumb I am holding your vagus nerve," he said calmly. "It runs from your brain to your heart and lungs. If I pinch it off, you'll be in big trouble. It's not easy to find – but I know exactly where it is. Do I make myself clear?"

"Yes." Tapper's eyes were bulging. Sledgeman moved forward, but Tapper gestured for him to keep back. The look in the young man's eyes was enough to convince Tapper not to mess with him.

"Now, let's try this again," said Alex. "I want to see Mickey. Do you have any problems with that?"

"No."

Alex released the huge man. Tapper John fell back, massaging his throat. Gabby let out a brief cackle of laughter. Tapper John snarled at him. Gabby made himself scarce.

Alex pushed the chapel door open and stepped inside. Tapper John and Sledgeman followed him in and stood with their backs to the door.

The chapel was large and ornate. White stone pillars

supported soaring arches. There were tall windows, high in the walls. Rows of empty wooden seats faced an empty altar. There was a stone pulpit. It was a strangely quiet and peaceful place to find in the middle of a prison.

Stone was sitting all alone towards the back of the chapel. He was staring up at the unreachable windows, his arms spread over the backs of two other chairs.

Alex moved softly across the floor and sat down directly behind him.

"Hello, Mr Stone," Alex said. "Praying for a miracle?"

Stone turned his head.

"Well, well. If it isn't one of Jack Cooper's brats," he said, his voice utterly humourless. "What's the problem: couldn't the big man come himself?" He turned, leaning over the back of his chair. "Of course not – I almost forgot – he'd never get his wheelchair up the stairs." Their eyes locked, Stone's brimming with hatred, Alex's icy and deadly calm. There was no way that Alex was going to give Stone the satisfaction of knowing how effective his jibes about DCS Cooper's disability were. Alex wouldn't rise to that particular bait.

"Jack Cooper set me up," Stone said after thirty futile seconds of eye-fencing with Alex. "I don't know anything about these crimes I'm supposed to have committed. I'm just a business man." His eyes narrowed. "I wouldn't hurt a fly," he said, his voice low and slow. "Unless it got in my way – and then..." His hand came slamming down on the back of his chair. "...I'd swat it. Do you get me, Mr Cox?"

Alex didn't turn a hair. He didn't even reply. Stone smiled coldly. "When you next see Jack, send him my best wishes. It's been over a year since he lost his wife, hasn't it? How is he bearing up all on his own? Oh, but he's not on his own, is he – he has a lovely daughter." The teeth bared in a graveyard smile. "The one who used to be a dancer."

A nerve twitched under Alex's right eye. Every muscle in his body ached to be unleashed on Stone, to beat him to the ground – to wipe that evil smirk off his face.

But he did nothing. With a supreme effort he kept his voice level. "Is there anything you want to tell me, Mr Stone?" he said tightly. "I'm here to give you one last chance to do yourself a favour."

Stone stared at him. "You mean, will I do a deal with you, like that treacherous rat Bryson?" he said. He laughed harshly. "Forget it, Cox. There won't be any deals." He stood up. "I'm due to meet with my solicitor," he said. "If I were you, Mr Cox, I'd say a few prayers before you go."

Stone walked heavy-footed to the doors. Sledgeman and Tapper John followed him out. The door slammed behind them.

✪

It was half an hour later.

Alex came gladly out of the stifling atmosphere of the prison and into the fresh air. He walked over to a row of parked cars.

He had to keep an appointment with Mickey Stone's solicitor.

He used a small electronic device to disable the alarm on Maurice Simms's red BMW. He opened the door with a master key and sat in the passenger seat. Then he waited.

Simms appeared about twenty minutes later.

He saw Alex. He hesitated. He looked as if he wanted to turn around and run. Alex beckoned him with one finger.

Simms got into the car. Twitchy and sweating.

"Well?" Alex said.

"I don't like this," he muttered. "If Mr Stone finds out that I've been talking to you people, do you know what he'll do to me?"

"I hadn't given it a single thought," Alex said.

Simms shot him a glance. "I want a better deal," he said.

"Nothing doing," said Alex. "I want to know Stone's escape plans, and I want to know them now." He turned and stared into the nervous man's eyes. "Talk."

Maurice Simms talked.

○

Danny whistled tunelessly to himself as he tinkered inside the MSU. The final tests with the slimline bugs had been a total success. He had handed them over to Alex a little while earlier. He had given clear instructions on what to do with them. Two would be sewn into Stone's clothing. A third would be slipped into the back of his watch. The switch would be made while Stone was in the dining hall that evening.

Danny smiled to himself. "And then, Mr Stone," he murmured. "You can go where you like, as fast as you like, and we'll be right there on your tail." He began to whistle again, gently probing a circuit with an instrument as fine as a cat's whisker.

"Danny?" A voice from the open back of the van.

Danny frowned. "Don't creep up on me," he said. "I'm working with delicate stuff in here."

"We've just had a call through from Alex," said the

35

agent. "Stone is making his move at midnight. The boss thinks we should be in place a couple of hours early, to be on the safe side."

Danny nodded. "That's cool," he said. "I just have a few more minutes work on this little gizmo."

The man stared at him. "What is that?" he said. "It looks like an espresso coffee maker."

Danny grinned widely. "Got it in one," he said. "Once I've wired it into the power, we'll have hot coffee on tap all night long." He chuckled. "How else am I going to keep awake so long after my bedtime?"

❂

Stansted Airport.

The Arrivals zone.

16:55.

The Arrivals screens showed that flight number FR222 – a Boeing 737 from Dublin Airport, had landed on schedule at 16:50.

Among the passengers on board the plane, was Mr Patrick Fitzgerald O'Connor, a wealthy and influential American businessman. Yesterday evening "Teflon Pat" O'Connor and his small staff had taken a flight from their home-town airport: Boston's Logan International Airport.

Flight EI136. Boston to Dublin Airport.

A flight straight from Logan to Heathrow would have been simpler and faster, but Mr O'Connor's advisers felt that a flight into Stansted would be more discreet under the circumstances.

Travelling with Mr O'Connor was a British man whose passport named him as Gerald Starkey. He was not an employee of Mr O'Connor. He was hoping to put some UK business Mr O'Connor's way.

Mr O'Connor and Mr Starkey strode towards the waiting crowd. Mr O'Connor's staff followed in their wake. A lawyer. A press agent. A personal assistant. A secretary. Two bodyguards.

They were met by a power-dressed woman carrying a clipboard. The board held several sheets of paper with the heading: Transatlantic Business Symposium.

The woman greeted the men and led them across the airport building towards the exit.

Gerald Starkey stepped out into the open air. His long black coat caught in the breeze. He looked around, smiling. He was tall and slim. His dark hair floated in the wind. He smoothed it with a quick movement of his hand. He was twenty-five years old. He strode alongside Teflon Pat O'Connor, towards a waiting stretch limousine.

They got into the car. Mr O'Connor's PA, and one of

the bodyguards entered with them. The other members of his staff got into a smaller car parked to the rear of the limousine.

"Let's go," said Mr O'Connor.

His PA knocked on the tinted glass divider. The chauffeur nodded. The engine purred.

The limousine glided out of the grounds of the airport, heading towards the M11. The Transatlantic Business Symposium was being held in the TravelStop Hotel in Harlow, Essex.

Patrick O'Connor turned to Gerald Starkey. "How does it feel to be back in the UK?" he asked.

"It feels great," said Starkey, his ice-blue eyes glittering as he stared out of the limousine's window. "It feels just great."

Chapter Three

Wormwood Scrubs Remand Wing.

Mickey Stone's cell.

23:33.

Mickey Stone was sitting in darkness on his narrow bunk. He was wearing an open shirt and trousers. There was just enough light filtering in through the barred window for him to be able to see the hands of his watch.

He had been sitting there for two hours. Not moving. Hunched over. Lifting his arm every few minutes to check the time. His fist was clenched around a small capsule, passed secretly to him by the prison doctor.

The doctor had been easy to intimidate. Mickey had sent Sledgeman. The doctor had rolled over in about thirty seconds.

Now all Mickey Stone had to do was swallow the capsule.

As easy as that.

Mickey Stone opened his fist and looked at the small white capsule. Uneasy.

He took a long, deep breath. Now or never.

He lifted his arm. He opened his mouth. He threw his head back and let the capsule slip between his teeth. He closed his mouth and swallowed dryly.

Two hard swallows to get rid of it.

He lay down on his bunk, staring at the ceiling.

Noises came drifting into his cell. Shouts. Bangs. Clangs. Echoing footsteps. Keys rattling. All the usual night-time prison noises. Except that they sounded sharper and louder than Mickey Stone had ever noticed before. Crowding in on him.

He began to sweat. He could feel his heart thundering in his chest. The blood pounded in his head. He began to breathe short, hard, sharp breaths. Dizzying.

A pain like the sudden blow of a sledgehammer struck him in the centre of his chest.

He bellowed in agony.

The sound of his own voice seemed to come from a huge distance.

He vaguely heard feet. Running. Keys clanking together.

A door opening. Light.

So much pain.

✪

00:03.

Alex stared at the gun in Mickey Stone's hand.

Stone had taken Alex's mobile with its hands-free kit. He had beaten the phone against a sharp corner of metal until it had fallen to pieces. And all the while his eyes had been on Alex, and the gun had been trained on a point in the centre of Alex's forehead.

Alex didn't move. His job wasn't to stop Mickey – it was to make sure Mickey didn't harm anyone in his bid for freedom. Alex's eyes flashed around the rolling interior of the ambulance. The doctor was a quivering mess. The older guard was tied and helpless on the floor. Barry Dean's wrists were tied behind his back.

The ambulance took a hard left turn. Alex tried to guess where they were being taken. North. Into Scrubs Lane. Towards Harlesden. Towards the M1 motorway and a quick route out of London.

That was when things began to go wrong.

Mickey glanced at the doctor. "Come here," he said. "Sit by me. Take my watch off." Looking puzzled, the doctor unstrapped the watch. "Open up the back," Stone said. "It unscrews."

The doctor did as he was told. A wafer-thin green disc with hair-fine metal filaments fell into Stone's waiting palm.

Alarm bells began to ring in Alex's head.

Stone lifted his hand to his mouth. He closed his teeth on the tracer bug and snapped it in two.

In the MSU, the first of the red lights winked suddenly out.

"Cut my collar open," Stone said to the doctor. "There's another one of those things in there. And there's a third one in the waistband of my trousers." He looked at Alex. "Just how stupid do you people think I am?" he said. "I knew Simms was whispering in your ears. I knew you were setting me up."

The ambulance took a lurch to the left.

Alex gave no sign of how his brain was racing to come up with a way out of this situation. They were heading west now. Going where?

"I've got people all over that prison," Stone said. "I was told about these tricky little devices of yours." His eyes grew cold. "So, you were going to let me out like a dog on a lead, were you? You were going to follow me with that white van of yours. I don't think so, Mr Cox."

The doctor held out the two remaining tracker bugs.

"Smash them," Stone snapped.

One broke – the other fell on the floor. Intact. It slid under the stretcher. Stone frowned at the doctor. "Get it, you fool," he said. The doctor went down on all fours. Searching.

Stone leaned towards Alex. "Like I was saying, I need some information." The gun hovered dangerously. "Where are you keeping Richard Bryson?"

The question came as a total shock to Alex.

In an instant, he realised the fatal flaw in their plan. They had assumed Mickey Stone would lead them straight to Eddie. Stone obviously had other ideas.

"I have no idea," Alex said calmly.

Stone's brutal face creased in thought. "Yes, you do," he said in a low voice. "But I think you'd rather take a bullet than tell me." He pursed his lips. "I wonder if I can come up with a solution?" His eyes turned to the young prison guard. "It's Barry, isn't it?" He smiled but his eyes were cold. "Let's you and me have a little chat, Barry."

Fear welled in the young guard's face.

Things were taking a bad turn.

PIC Control.

The Surveillance Room hummed with electronic equipment. Tara Moon was at the mike. Jack Cooper sat rigid at her side. Maddie was hunched in a chair, staring at the receiver. Danny's last message had hit them like ice water.

All three bugs had been lost. Not a systems failure, Danny had been sure of that. They had been found and smashed.

There was only one explanation.

Stone had known about the bugs.

Jack Cooper leaned into the mike. "Danny? Have you got visual on them still?"

"No. We've lost them. We're at the junction with Scrubs Lane. They could have gone either way."

Maddie had street maps flicking across her computer screen. "A north turn would take them to the M1," she said. "South leads down to Hammersmith and the M4."

"If they want the quickest route out of London," Tara said, "they'd go for the M1."

"Give me an open channel," Jack Cooper said to Tara. "I want to talk to the two cars trailing the MSU."

Tara flipped some switches.

"OK," Jack Cooper said into the mike. "DS Marsh – I want you to head for Hammersmith. DS Slater, you make for the M1. We've got to find that ambulance."

"What do we do when we find them, Boss?" came Slater's voice. "Do we just track them, or do we stop them?"

"Wait!" Jack Cooper's voice was a harsh growl. He sat in his wheelchair, staring at nothing.

Maddie bit her lip. She knew the terrible decision he had to make. To bring Operation Babysitter to a crashing halt by picking Mickey Stone up; or to let things run their course and pray that Stone didn't give them the slip.

Maddie stared at her father. How does a person make a decision like that? It was impossible. She felt like shouting: *Dad! You've got to get Alex out of there! He could be killed!* But she bit down on her lip and kept silent.

Jack Cooper leaned into the mike.

"Find them, but keep well back," he said. "Keep them in sight, but take no other action without specific orders from me."

Maddie felt a coldness in her chest. There wasn't going to be a rescue attempt. Alex was on his own.

Chapter Four

Mickey Stone was sitting next to Barry Dean. The gun was still trained on Alex.

"What's a young lad like you doing in a situation like this, Barry?" Stone asked gently. His arm was around the young guard's shoulders, his fingers digging in.

Alex hoped that Barry wouldn't do anything that might get him killed.

"Are you married, Barry?" Stone asked. "Wife and kids?"

"Yes." Barry Dean's voice was thin and breathless.

"Any pictures?" Stone asked.

Barry Dean nodded. "In my wallet. In my breast pocket."

"May I see?"

The young guard nodded. Stone pulled the wallet out of his shirt pocket. He opened it and took out a small snapshot. He looked at it. Smiling.

"Adorable," Stone said. "What are their names?"

"My wife's name is Marie." The terrified voice was almost inaudible. "The girls are Sally and Briony. Sally is four. Briony is just coming up to two years old."

Stone flipped the picture over and showed it to Alex.

"Don't they look like a nice, happy family, Mr Cox?"

Alex stared at the picture. Mum on a couch with the two girls crawling over her. All smiling. "They look very nice," Alex said.

"Do you read bedtime stories to Sally and Briony, Barry?" Stone asked. Alex knew there was something bad coming.

"Yes," Barry Dean said. "When I get the chance."

"Lovely," Stone said. "Just lovely." He crushed the picture in his fist. He turned the gun and pressed it to the side of the young guard's head. Barry closed his eyes, pale as death.

"Mr Stone... you can't..." the doctor's voice protested weakly.

"Shut it!" Stone snapped. He looked at Alex. "Tell

me where Bryson is or Barry won't be telling Sally and Briony any more bedtime stories."

Alex didn't speak for the space of two heartbeats.

But he couldn't risk it.

"OK," he said. "You win. Put the gun down. I'll tell you what you want to know."

Stone smiled. "Of course you will, Mr Cox. Of course you will."

✪

The ambulance had stopped.

But where? There hadn't been time for them to have gone far. They had turned off to the left somewhere along Scrubs Lane. Alex tried to visualise the area. There were playing fields. There was a sports stadium. There was Wormwood Scrubs Common.

Alex guessed what was going on. Stone was going to ditch the cumbersome ambulance for something less obvious. A fast getaway car.

Stone had ordered the doctor to bind Alex. His arms were locked behind his back, strapped tight at the wrists and elbows. His legs were tied at his ankles and knees. If he tried to move, he'd wind up on his face on the floor of the ambulance. There was no good way out of this situation.

But at least he'd prevented a tragedy in there. Stone

had stopped threatening Barry Dean the moment Alex had told him where Bryson was being held.

The back doors of the ambulance sprang open. Alex had to adjust his position or he would have fallen out. He turned and looked out into the night. Now he knew exactly where they were.

The long roof of the Linford Christie Stadium cut across the sky over to their left. Away to their right and out of Alex's line of vision, stood Wormwood Scrubs Prison. They had virtually doubled back on themselves. PIC cars would be racing towards the motorways, and they were tucked out of sight, not much more than five hundred metres from the prison. Some joke!

Louie looked into the ambulance.

"Nice work, Louie," Stone said. He got to his feet and made his way down out of the vehicle. He took a huge breath and stretched. Alex fought down a surge of anger and frustration as he saw the big man's fists lift to the dark sky in triumph.

"Fresh air!" Stone said. "It smells good, Louie." He turned towards the ambulance. Smiling. "I'll have my watch back, Doc," he said.

The doctor scrambled down to the ground. He handed the watch over. Mickey Stone strapped it on his wrist with slow deliberation. "How long?" he asked Louie.

 49

"Any time now, Boss," Louie said.

Stone walked to and fro, clearly enjoying being able to stretch his legs, tilting his head back as he snorted in the cool night air.

Alex heard the sound of a car approaching. He looked down along the road. Headlights shone brightly in the darkness.

The car slowed. Alex was dazzled by the headlights – he could see nothing beyond them. The car stopped about ten metres away from the ambulance. There was the sound of a door opening. A dark shape moved forward.

"Hello, Mr Stone," called a voice.

"Hello Chas," Stone responded, walking towards the car. "Nice to see you again."

Mickey Stone's ride to revenge and freedom had arrived. There was nothing that Alex could do to prevent him from climbing into that car and disappearing into the night.

☒

Danny crouched in the back of the MSU. They were at the roadside at the eastern end of Du Cane Road. On tenterhooks. Waiting for a positive sighting.

One thing that Danny had learned from working under Jack Cooper was the importance of improvisation – of thinking on your feet. If there's a foul-up, try something else. Keep pushing. Don't quit working until you find a way through.

Mickey Stone had sussed them out. Alex was out of contact and in a whole world of trouble. The missing ambulance had to be found – and quick.

Danny brought an aerial photograph of the area up on the screen of his laptop. He was listening intently to the messages coming through his headset – constantly moving faders to change channels.

Silence from Control.

Bad news from the two cars.

There was no sign of the ambulance.

Danny's fingers flicked over the keyboard. He pulled up a Metropolitan Police site. He punched in the password. Now he had instant visual access to a whole network of CCTV street surveillance cameras. His fingers pumped up and down on his mouse, changing cameras with machine-gun rapidity.

"Where are you?" he whispered to himself. "Come on – you know you want me to find you."

Nothing.

A report came in from Slater. "We're in Willesden. We're making for the North Circular. No sign of them. We're chasing shadows. They must have gone the other way."

51

Danny shook his head. "I don't think so," he muttered to himself off-mike. The grainy grey street scenes whipped by on-screen. The ambulance was nowhere. It was as if the ground had just opened up and swallowed it.

"Unless..." Danny flipped back to the aerial photograph. He clicked on "zoom" with a sudden flash of insight. He could see the prison. Hammersmith Hospital. Green playing fields. Around the back of the playing fields, was the unmistakable outline of the Linford Christie Stadium. And to the north, the wide green expanse of the common.

"If I was in a big old ambulance and I was being chased by an NSX and an RX7, I wouldn't try to make a run for it," Danny muttered to himself. "I'd tuck myself into a corner, somewhere real close by, and I'd just watch those suckers go whizzing past!"

He sat up and called to his driver. "Gina – the heck with sitting around doing nothing. Hit the gas – we're out of here."

Chapter Five

Now that Alex's eyes were used to the dazzle of the headlights, he could see that the getaway vehicle was a two-seater sports car: a yellow Lotus Elise. *Good choice*, Alex thought ruefully. The car was fast and light with an aerodynamic aluminium frame. Zero to 100 kph in 4.5 seconds. It could easily make 200 kph on a clear road.

Mickey Stone and the other man were standing at the front of the car. Shaking hands like old buddies. Alex couldn't see the driver's face, but he was able to make a good guess at who he was: Chas Lennox, a Stonecor foot soldier from way back. PIC had a file on him. He was a small-time crook. He had been Stone's chauffeur before his boss had been locked up.

The doctor approached the two men.

Mickey turned to him. "Do you want something, Doc?" he asked.

The doctor's voice was hesitant. "You promised me – we had a deal – enough money to get me out of the country..."

Mickey Stone looked coldly at him. "That was before I knew how much your pills were going to hurt, Doc," he said smoothly. "You gave me pain – it's only fair that I give you pain back, right?"

The doctor took a step backwards, suddenly realising his danger.

"I helped you," he said, his voice wavering.

"You'll get your reward in heaven, Doc." Mickey stepped forward suddenly and a blunt fist hammered into the doctor's face, striking with pile-driver force. The doctor fell back and rolled on to his side, both hands clutching at his face.

Alex's eyes narrowed. That had been nasty. Unnecessary.

"Let's go," barked Stone. "Louie – over here."

Stone and Chas Lennox got into the car. Louie went loping over to the passenger side. The motor gunned.

Stone looked up at Louie. "You know what to do," he

said. He looked expressionlessly towards the ambulance. Louie nodded.

The car did a rapid three-point turn.

The doctor staggered to his feet. He stumbled after the car. He snatched hold of the passenger door handle. It didn't open. There was a snarl of gears and a squeal of rubber as Chas revved the engine.

The car bolted – the doc still clinging to the door handle. Alex winced as the man was dragged off his feet. He was towed along for a few metres before he lost his grip. He rolled on the ground. The car sped off into the night.

Louie stood at the open back doors of the ambulance. He looked in at the three bound men for a moment then disappeared.

Alex checked out the guards. "Is everyone OK?" he asked.

The older guard nodded grimly.

"Yes," Barry Dean breathed. "What happens now?"

"We wait for the cavalry to arrive," Alex said. He assumed Louie was already gone. He stared out along the road. The doctor wasn't moving.

Alex heard sounds from the cab of the ambulance. He frowned, puzzled. What was Louie still doing there?

A couple of minutes later, Louie reappeared,

carrying two petrol cans. He heaved the cans up into the ambulance. Alex's heart missed a beat. A cold terror drained down through him.

Louie climbed up into the ambulance. He picked up one of the cans and twisted the long-nosed tube at one end. He tipped the can and a wash of bluish liquid flooded over the floor. The smell of petrol filled the ambulance.

Louie moved back and forth, pouring petrol over everything in there.

"Louie," Alex said. "There's no need for this."

Louie looked at him. "I've got my orders," he said. "It's nothing personal."

"At least let the boy go," the older guard said, nodding towards Barry Dean.

"Sorry," said Louie in a calm, reasonable voice. "No can do. I'd like to help, really I would, but Mr Stone's orders were to torch the ambulance with you guys inside." He shrugged. "I think he wants to make an example of you – know what I mean?"

"Listen to me carefully, Louie," Alex said, trying to keep the fear out of his voice. "I've seen your file. You're just small fry. Smash and grab. Petty burglary." He raised the pitch of his voice. "This is different, Louie. If you do this, everything changes for you. For ever. No matter how you look at it, Louie, what you're about to do here is cold-blooded murder."

Louie stopped. He looked at Alex. His face thoughtful.

Alex pinned him with his piercing eyes. "If you kill us, you're going to be on the run for the rest of your life," he said. "My people won't rest until they find you. And they will find you, Louie – I can promise you that."

Louie shook his head. "I don't see how," he said. "Who's going to tell them it was me? You'll all be toast!"

He jumped down from the back of the ambulance and walked towards the doctor.

Alex looked at the two guards. It was a moment beyond words. His attempt at reasoning with the man had failed. They were going to be burned alive in there. It was too horrible to comprehend.

Alex watched as Louie half carried, half dragged the doctor to the ambulance. The man was only semi-conscious, his clothes filthy and torn – his face grazed and bleeding. Louie hauled him up into the ambulance and laid him on his back in the narrow aisle.

He jumped down again. He picked up the second of the petrol cans and began to pour more of the deadly, stinking fuel over the ground under and to the rear of the vehicle.

Alex tried one last time. "This isn't necessary, Louie!" he said. "Don't do it."

Louie reached for the doors and swung them together. The last thing Alex saw was an apologetic smile as the ambulance doors banged shut.

"Oh my God," whispered Barry Dean.

Alex closed his eyes, psyching himself up for one last, supreme effort. He tensed his body, straining and writhing against his bonds. If he could only get a hand free. His muscles screamed with the effort. His nostrils filled with the stench of the petrol. A small voice in his brain told him that it was pointless, that there was no way he could get himself free.

Alex ignored that voice. He would struggle to get loose until the very last second of his life.

Louie threw the empty petrol can under the back of the ambulance. He felt in his trouser pocket. His fingers closed around an oblong of metal. A Zippo lighter.

Louie stepped back from the petrol-soaked ground.

He held a long screw of paper in his other hand. He flicked up the lid of the Zippo with his thumb. He ran his thumb across the wheel. There was a spark. A bright white flame leapt up. Louie held the end of the screw of paper into the flame. It caught, and a bigger, yellowish flame began to grow on the shrivelling taper.

Louie waited until the paper was burning along half its length.

The flame was hungry. Shadows flickered over Louie's face.

The apologetic smile was still there. His eyes reflected the flame as he held the burning screw of paper at arm's length and prepared to drop it on to the petrol-soaked ground.

It was nothing personal.

✪

The yellow Lotus Elise sped towards Scrubs Lane.

"How's things, Chas?" Stone asked as he clipped his seat belt.

"It's all been sorted, Boss," said Chas Lennox. "Just the way you asked."

"Good lad," Stone said. He leaned back into the leather seat. "But there's been a slight change of plan."

Chas glanced at his boss, surprise registering on his face.

"I want you to take me to Shepherd's Bush," Stone said.

Chas Lennox frowned. "You should get out of town, Boss – like we arranged – as fast as possible."

"I intend to," said Stone. "But first, I want to pay a surprise call on an old friend of mine."

"Whatever you say, Boss."

Chas turned the sports car to the right, feeding his way into the southbound traffic along Wood Lane. He drove fast and hard, slipping in and out of the slower vehicles. They shot under the overpass of the Westway.

Stone smiled to himself. Just a few more minutes, and that big-mouthed rat Bryson would learn exactly what it meant to turn traitor on Mickey Stone.

Chapter Six

Danny leaned over Gina's shoulder as she drove the MSU north along Scrubs Lane.

"Turn left here," he said.

"Are you sure?" Gina replied. "This just takes us around the back of the prison."

"Trust me," Danny said. "I'm working on a hunch."

Gina spun the wheel and the MSU did a fast, lurching turn. The headlights lit up the road ahead. About 250 metres away in the darkness, Danny saw a big, square shape.

"That's them!" Gina said. "Nice guess, Danny." She flipped a switch to put the headlights on full beam.

Danny peered into the night. "What the heck...?"

A figure – standing near the back of the ambulance. A man. His head was turned over his shoulder. He was staring down the road at the approaching white van. Something was on fire in one of his hands.

Gina put her foot down.

The MSU thundered forwards – aiming straight at the man.

He threw the burning thing as he ran.

The screw of paper fluttered, flaming to the ground. It sputtered and shrivelled and went out only a metre from the edge of the spreading pool of petrol.

Danny threw himself into the back of the MSU. He grabbed a mike, flipping switches.

"We've found the ambulance," he said. "It's at the Linford Christie Stadium. We could use some backup!"

The MSU came to a shuddering stop. Gina leapt out of the cab and sprinted after the fleeing man. She brought him down within twenty metres.

Danny clambered out and ran to the ambulance. He sniffed. Petrol.

The significance of the burning paper hit him.

He tore the back door of the ambulance open.

He let out a gasp of relief as he saw three desperate faces staring out at him. A fourth man lay on the floor.

"Are you guys OK?" he panted.

"Get a car over to Stanlake Mansions," Alex shouted. "Stone is after Bryson!"

Danny stood staring up at his colleague for a moment – but only for a moment. He turned on his heel and raced back to the MSU.

✪

Shepherd's Bush.

An upper room in Stanlake Mansions.

A discarded pizza box lay on the floor. Uneaten slices of pizza cooled and congealed. Loud dance music came pounding through the wall – the electronic drums beating out a deafening 120-bpm rhythm.

Bryson was spread-eagled against the wall, hammering with both hands. Shouting uselessly against the tidal wave of music.

Alice Chang was back on duty. She had to put up with the noisy music and with Bryson's unhinged behaviour until six a.m. She looked at her watch. It wasn't even half past twelve. She had to cope with this madness for another five and a half hours.

"Richard!" she shouted. "They can't hear you. Why don't you lie down."

Bryson stared round at her. His eyes were red-rimmed and wild. He was at breaking point.

He threw himself on his narrow, unmade bed, and

dragged a pillow over his head.

Alice Chang sipped coffee.

The music stopped so suddenly that it was almost a shock.

Bryson sat up, staring at the wall. He looked at his minder. Alice Chang shrugged.

"Get some sleep, Richard."

He lay down again, his eyes wide – staring up at the ceiling.

A small noise broke the silence. A creak. Outside the door of the room.

Alice Chang turned her head towards the door – instantly suspicious and alert.

Bryson sat up again, staring at the door with a look of alarm on his face.

Alice Chang's mobile phone rang. She reached for it automatically, her eyes still on the locked door.

The door to the room burst open at the precise moment the music blared forth once more. A huge surge of movement and noise in the strange stillness of the room.

Bryson's mouth stretched open in a silent scream of absolute terror.

Alice Chang sprang out of the armchair as a heavy-set figure filled the doorway.

Chapter Seven

Alex brought his silver Ducati motorbike around the curve of Stanlake Road. Danny was on the pillion seat. They could see Stanlake Mansions: the ugly, run-down block where Richard Bryson was being held.

It had been the work of a few seconds for Danny to cut Alex free of his bonds. Then there had been the desperate run to the prison forecourt to get to Alex's motorbike.

The message had gone out to the two PIC cars: *Get to Stanlake Mansions. Stone on his way there. Bryson must be moved.* But DS Slater was driving north on the Edgware Road – a long way now from Shepherd's Bush – heading in the wrong direction. The other car was on the Great West Road, also heading the wrong way.

Alex slammed on the brakes and the motorbike came to a skidding halt. There were no other PIC vehicles there yet. Alex and Danny were first on the scene.

Danny let out a hiss, his fingers tightening on Alex's shoulder. A sleek shape came hurtling from a side street next to the mansion block. A Lotus Elise, its soft-top closed, its yellow paintwork shining in the streetlights. The car sped towards them for a split second before the brakes were applied.

Alex shielded his eyes from the dazzle of full headlights. He knew that car. Suddenly it drove backwards down the road at high speed. Mounting the pavement, the driver executed a breathtaking 180 degree turn – the gleaming bonnet whipping round. There was a powerful roar and a screech of burning rubber. An instant later, the sports car was speeding away from them.

Alex reacted instantly. The Ducati's powerful engine snarled as Alex sent the motorbike in headlong pursuit of the car. Danny clung on grimly, his eyes narrowed to slits against the lash of the wind.

❌

DS Marsh led his team up the dark, narrow stairway. They were all armed. They knew Mickey Stone had a gun: they had to assume he would use it if he was cornered.

They heard loud dance music. It seemed to be coming from the next building along.

DS Marsh frowned. This wasn't good. The noise would mask any other sounds.

Was Stone already there? Were they walking into the barrel of a loaded gun?

Marsh was the first to come up to the top floor. He pressed himself against the wall. The doorway to the room where Bryson was being kept was wide open.

Bad.

Marsh slid along the wall, his gun held ready in two hands. His team of three followed on, keeping low, keeping flat, keeping safe. The noise of the beat-heavy music blotted out every other sound.

The doorway gaped ominously.

DS Marsh slid along the wall. He straightened up at the side of the door. He waited until his team got into place. He took deep breaths, steadying his nerves. He nodded to his team. He threw himself through the doorway.

The room was a wreck. Alice Chang lay face down on the floor, her mobile phone only centimetres away from her outstretched hand. She had been given no time to answer Danny's call. It had come too late to do her any good. Stone had come down on her like a ton of bricks.

DS Marsh knelt at her side. He turned her over.

She was alive. Just.

He looked up at the three agents who had entered the room in his wake.

"Put a call through," he shouted. "We need an ambulance. And tell Control that we were too late. Tell them Bryson is gone."

✪

Danny had lost all track of where they were. The maze of streets flashed by in a wind-torn blur. Alex was pursuing the speeding Lotus with absolute determination. Operation Babysitter might be a bust, but Alex was going to minimise the fallout. Stone was not going to get away from them.

Danny clung on grimly as Alex took another corner at stomach-turning speed. The motorbike leaned hard into the curve. The sports car was a shining fist in the road ahead. Lampposts flicked past. Road after road twisted and meshed as they hurtled through a tangle of backstreets.

Danny prayed silently as the air whipped past his ears. Alex was an ace driver, but at this speed even he would be in trouble if anything unexpected happened.

All of Alex's concentration was focused on the tail-lights of the Lotus. He was gradually gaining on the sports car. As street by frantic street was left in their wake, the gap between them diminished. The sports car took yet another screaming, tyre-shredding turn.

Alex rounded the bend. He saw the Lotus slip into a narrow alley between high walls.

He came to a skidding halt at the mouth of the narrow wedge of darkness. He had no idea where this led. The alley was only just wide enough to take the car. Alex throttled up and aimed his motorbike into the dark slot.

The walls shot by. Alex could see the tail-lights of the car, staring back like demon eyes. The motorbike burst out into a wide area of concrete, hemmed in on all sides by tall brick walls. The Lotus was at the far end of the darkened concrete expanse. It wasn't moving. It was sideways on to them. They could hear the engine being revved. It sounded like the threatening growl of some dangerous animal brought to bay.

"There's no other way out," Danny shouted. "We got 'em!"

Alex nodded, breathing hard and fast. He watched the car through narrowed eyes.

Now what?

The car moved slowly along the wall. It began to turn towards them. The roaring of the engine filled the night. The car was face-on to them now – its low bonnet pointing directly at the only exit from the trap that it had caught itself in.

Alex's heart raced.

There was a moment's pause.

"Alex? What...?"

The car leaped forwards with a roar.

"Hang on to me," Alex said, his voice tight and clipped.

The sports car rocketed towards them. The driver intended to get out of that trap, even if it meant driving straight over the motorbike that blocked the exit.

Alex twisted the throttle. The Ducati pounced forward. He crouched low, steering straight between the headlights of the rapidly approaching car.

Danny let out a moan as he saw what Alex was doing. He clung on to him. He shut his eyes tight. He waited for the inevitable killing slam into the front of the car.

Alex was playing chicken with a souped-up sports car with a 1.8 litre, 16-valve engine. Danny had a horrible feeling that Alex wasn't going to be the first one to swerve.

He was right.

But Alex wasn't being reckless. He was taking the only option open to him. He wasn't going to sit there and wait for the car to run into him. He was going to meet it half way. He was going to test the driver's nerve.

The stretch of concrete dividing the two speeding vehicles rapidly shortened.

They were a split second from a head-on crash when the Lotus careered aside. Alex reacted instantly, turning the handlebars just enough so that his leg grazed the car's front bumper as they passed each other.

He slammed on the brakes.

The driver of the Lotus had miscalculated. The side of the car scraped along a wall, spilling a comet's tail of sparks along the concrete. The car pulled away from the wall. But it was still going too fast. As it turned, two wheels left the ground.

There was a scream of metal and a dull, hollow thud as the Lotus flipped on to its side. It scraped along for a few metres before coming to a halt against the wall.

Danny and Alex ran towards the upended car. The headlights blazed. That meant the electrics were still on. One spark in the wrong place and the car would go up like a bomb.

71

A figure crawled through the ripped roof-covering.

Alex caught hold of him. It was Chas Lennox. Bloodied but apparently not seriously injured.

Petrol poured from the ruptured fuel tank.

Danny saw a tongue of dark yellow fire. He yelled out a warning.

The three of them threw themselves to the ground as the car erupted into flames.

They crawled away from the intense heat.

"Who else was in there?" Alex shouted.

Lennox wiped blood out of his eyes, staring back at the blazing car.

"No one but me," he said. He laughed. "Sorry, guys, but you've been had!"

The truth hit Alex and Danny at the same moment.

The car was a decoy.

Its whole purpose had been to lead them away from wherever Stone had gone. It had worked perfectly.

Danny got dizzily to his feet. He dusted down his clothes and took out his mobile. Control needed to know what had happened.

It was not a call he was looking forward to.

Chapter Eight

PIC Control.

Maddie came back into the Surveillance Room, carrying three cups of coffee on a tray. It wasn't her job to fetch drinks, but the tension had been so oppressive in that small room, she had been glad to get out for a few moments to catch her breath.

The door closed behind her. She stood absolutely still, listening to the urgent voice on the receiver. It was DS Marsh.

"We're too late. Bryson is gone. We have an agent down. We're going to need blanket backup over here if we're going to find Stone."

"How is Chang?" Jack Cooper barked.

had a bad bang on the head. I've called an
e." DS Marsh's voice cracked with anger and
frustration. "This is a disaster, Boss!"

A red light flashed. "I'm putting you on hold,
Michael," Tara said. She flipped channels.

Danny's voice was breathless and desperate.

Maddie silently placed the cups of coffee at Tara's
and her father's elbows. She sat down, listening intently
to Danny's report.

Another failure. It was beginning to look as if Stone
had tricked them at every point.

Jack Cooper leaned into the mike. "Danny? I'll send
a car. Get what you can out of Lennox."

Danny's voice was dull. "Will do, Boss – just as soon
as he quits laughing at us!"

The line was cut.

Tara got to work, calling up reinforcements. She had
a busy night ahead of her: picking up the pieces of
Operation Babysitter, hoping against hope that they
could throw a net over London tight enough to catch
Mickey Stone.

Maddie looked at her father. His face was pale and
drawn, his shoulders bowed. Maddie's forehead creased
with concern – she could see despair in his eyes. She had
never seen that look before. It scared her.

Ten slow seconds crawled by. Tara's voice filled the room as she marshalled and coordinated PIC's resources.

Jack Cooper took a long breath and lifted his head. The despair was gone. He turned his chair and headed for the door.

Maddie stood up and followed him out into the corridor. If he heard her, he made no sign. She walked along behind his wheelchair, wanting to be close to him but not knowing what to say. His plans were in ruins. What could she say to comfort or support him at such a moment? Nothing. All she could do was be at his side.

He went into his private office. He moved to the window and stared out at the city lights. The dome of St Paul's Cathedral and the gothic spires of the Houses of Parliament were illuminated against the night sky.

She stood at his side.

Her father looked up at her.

Their eyes met. Maddie swallowed hard, desperately worried about him.

Jack Cooper turned his wheelchair to the desk and picked up his phone.

"Put me through to the Home Secretary," he said.

Maddie glanced at the wall clock. 00:53. She was surprised how the time had sped by. She felt drained and hollow. It was a terrible feeling. She never wanted to feel that way again.

Her father looked up at her. "I think I'd better do this alone," he said gently.

She nodded.

Maddie left the office, turned and walked slowly away.

❽

Maddie lay in her bed. Unable to sleep. Tired to the bone, but wide awake. She looked at her bedside clock. 03:21. Would this horrible night never end?

She heard the sharp metal click of a key. The sound of a door opening. Quiet voices. Her father had finally come home. Who was with him?

Maddie sat up. She held her breath, straining to hear.

Her father's voice, soft from the hallway: "The D-notice should give us some breathing space."

He had set up a D-notice – a complete news blackout. Maddie could understand the sense in that. It would give them some time before the newspapers and the TV networks splashed the news of Mickey Stone's escape all over the country.

Her father's voice again: "Have you alerted the ports? He might try to get out of the country."

Tara Moon's voice. "It's all under control, sir. Airports. Ports. All exit points. All we can do now is wait – and you need to get some sleep."

Her father: "The debrief starts at six a.m. – sharp! I want everyone there. We need to organise some damage control."

Tara Moon: "Leave it to me."

"Pick me up at five forty-five."

The front door to their apartment clicked shut. Maddie listened to the faint sound of her father's wheelchair moving along the hallway. A door opened and closed.

Silence.

Maddie lay back in bed.

There was going to be a debriefing meeting at six in the morning – and everyone involved in Operation Babysitter had to be there. Everyone except Maddie, apparently. Her father was going to let her sleep through it.

Maddie had other ideas.

Chapter Nine

05:45.

The streets of London were cool and bright as Maddie drove her red Vespa to the corner of Bloomsbury Street and made the turn into New Oxford Street. The curved tower of concrete and glass that was the Centrepoint building lifted high into the pale sky. The sun reflected in its upper windows. The roads were busy, although the rush hour was still more than an hour away.

She parked and secured her motor scooter, and walked in through the glass doors. The door guard checked her pass. She walked through the security arch. Seconds later, she was in the lift, being taken up to the penthouse offices of Police Investigation Command.

With only a couple of hours sleep the previous night, Maddie's body felt leaden with the lack of real rest, but her mind was sharp and alert.

The red light was on over the Briefing Room door. She slipped quietly into the room and sat down next to Danny.

Her father was at the other end of the room, seated under a screen on which a map of the Greater London area was displayed. Everyone who had been involved in Operation Babysitter was there. The mood was sombre but not defeated.

Jack Cooper saw Maddie. A faint smile touched his lips – so much for letting his daughter sleep. He should have known better. He acknowledged her with a brief nod.

"The D-notice should keep the media off our backs for forty-eight hours," Jack Cooper said, "but it's not going to stop the news spreading by word of mouth. We've been given a little breathing space – but that's all." His keen eyes scanned the room. "It goes without saying that the Home Secretary is climbing the walls right now. And I've had a message from the head of Special Branch – *offering assistance.*"

A murmur ran through the room. It was well known that certain high-ranking officers in Special Branch believed that PIC should be under their control.

"I said thanks but no thanks," Jack Cooper growled. He smiled grimly. "Bad news travels fast on the police grapevine. The object of this meeting is to generate some good news." He looked to one side. "Tara? Situation report, please."

Tara stood up. Maddie guessed from the pallor of her face that she probably hadn't slept. "Our priority is to track Stone and Bryson down – and as soon as this meeting is over, most of you will be sent out to hunt for them," she said. "But we also need to find out where the crime summit is taking place. Everything we have heard so far suggests it's going to happen soon." Her piercing green eyes glittered. "Find the summit and we have a good chance of finding Stone."

A voice spoke from the body of the room. "Do you think Bryson might already be dead?"

Jack Cooper shook his head. "If Stone wanted Bryson dead, he'd have done the job in the safe house," he said. "No – we have to assume that Stone is keeping Bryson alive for some reason."

"What about Chas Lennox?" Alex asked. "Have we managed to get anything useful out of him yet?"

"I'm putting you and Tara on to that," Jack Cooper said. "He's had a few hours in the cells at Charing Cross to do some thinking. I want you to get over there and interview him. Find out exactly what he knows." He lifted his head. "Meanwhile, I want every available field agent out there on the streets. Danny – do the rounds of all your informants. We're going to find out where that summit is taking place." His voice was steely. "I expect to have the information on my desk today. Get busy!"

The room cleared rapidly.

Tara and Jack Cooper had their heads together, talking strategy. Maddie stood close by. Waiting.

Her father looked round at her.

"What do you want me to do?" she asked. She was the only PIC agent without clear orders.

"I need you here – coordinating all incoming reports," her father said. "You will be the focal point and information distribution source for the whole operation. Keep everyone updated regularly." He looked keenly at her. "This is important, Maddie. I need you to be on the ball."

She nodded. "I will be."

✪

PIC Control.

11:20.

Maddie clicked on SEND and another batch of rapidly edited reports flashed through to the computer terminals of every section leader in the building. She had been working flat out for hours. Breakfast had been a cheese roll, eaten at her desk while she typed with her free hand. Every now and then, someone brought her coffee. She drank without even tasting the stuff. She was entirely focused on her work. She didn't even have the time to realise how desperately tired her body was getting. Sleep would have to wait – right now, she was living on borrowed energy reserves. Working on the raw edge of her nerves.

The field reports had a grim similarity to them. No sightings. No new information. Nothing to tell. Over and out.

Stone and Bryson seemed to have vanished without trace.

"Hi, Maddie – how's it going?" Danny's voice on her headset.

"It's crazy over here," Maddie said. "Everyone's running around the place, but nothing's happening. What about you?"

"Zero so far," Danny said. "Have you heard anything

from Alex?"

"No. Nothing." Maddie looked at the time display on her screen. "They must have been in with Lennox for hours now, but I haven't heard a word."

"Let me know if anything breaks."

"Will do." The connection with Danny was terminated.

Maddie typed and the all-too-familiar words scrolled out on-screen:

Agent Bell – 11:29. Negative report.

✪

Charing Cross Police Station – Agar Street, London WC2.

Interview Room.

In attendance: PIC agent Tara Moon, PIC agent Alex Cox, Charles Lennox, Peter Lowden – solicitor.

Tara and Alex sat on one side of the white table. Chas Lennox and his solicitor sat opposite. Between them, the double tape machine was running. The interview had been in progress for several hours. Alex felt that he and Tara were getting nowhere slowly. Lennox was stonewalling them at every turn.

Chas Lennox was lolling back in his chair, his expression amused, his eyes insolent. His solicitor leaned forwards, hands clasped on the tabletop.

"My client has been nothing but cooperative," he said in a clipped voice. "He has admitted his role in the escape of Mr Stone and he has informed you that he was acting under duress and in fear of his life. As my client clearly knows nothing more on this matter, may I suggest we end this interview?"

Tara ignored him. She was gazing steadily at Lennox. He held her eyes for half a minute before he had to look away.

"Listen, Chas," Alex said. "No one is going to believe you helped Mickey because you were frightened of him. Do us all a favour, and stop messing us around."

Lennox spread his hands. "I'm really sorry, guys," he said with a shrug. "But I can't help you. I don't know anything." He grinned.

"Stop wasting our time," Tara said, her voice cold and hard. "We want to know where Stone is, and we want to know now. You're not going anywhere until we find out."

Lennox put a finger to his temple. "It's hard to remember if he told me anything important," he said. He frowned. "There was something about a flight to Ibiza." He smiled. "Great nightlife, so I hear." He winked at Tara. "Ever been there?"

Tara stared him down without speaking.

"I guess not," Lennox muttered, his eyes lowered. "Don't s'pose it's quite your scene, is it?" He laughed, but the laugh was uneasy.

"We're willing to do a deal with you, Chas," Alex said.

Lennox's eyes flashed. "Oh, I bet you are," he said. He leaned towards his solicitor. They spoke together – head-to-head – in subdued voices.

"My client would be happy to do everything he can to help you," said Peter Lowden. "On the condition that all charges against him are dropped."

"No," said Tara.

Lennox's eyes narrowed to surly slits. "Either I walk, or you get nothing."

Alex looked at him. Lennox was cool now – lounging back in his seat – in control. He could afford to keep them dangling. But every minute they lost in trying to squeeze information out of him, took them further away from any chance of recapturing Mickey Stone.

For the moment, Chas Lennox was holding all the cards.

And he knew it.

Chapter Ten

Tara and Alex were in the corridor outside the Briefing Room. The interview had been broken off. The tape machine had been stopped. Lennox and his solicitor were still in the room. Tara had sent in a uniformed officer to keep an eye on them while she and Alex discussed the situation.

"The bottom line is that he can afford to play games," Tara said. "And we can't."

Alex stared at the closed door of the interview room. "He knows exactly where Stone is," he said. "You can bet on that."

"Of course he does," said Tara. "The question is – how do we get him to open up?" She frowned. "I need to know what we can offer him." She took out her mobile and speed-dialled. She was one of the few people who could get direct access to DCS Cooper. He picked up almost immediately.

Tara gave him a rapid appraisal of their progress so far.

Alex walked edgily up and down while Tara and Jack Cooper talked. He wasn't good at this kind of thing. He had real problems with sitting for hours with a man who just laughed in his face. A session with Lennox on a jujitsu mat was more Alex's style. Pity it wasn't an option.

"OK, sir. I'll see what I can do." Tara snapped her phone shut. She looked at Alex. "We try one more bluff," she said. "If he doesn't go for it, we give him what he wants."

"He walks?" said Alex. "Me and Danny could have been pavement pizza because of that guy."

Tara shrugged. "That's the way it goes."

They went back into the interview room.

Lennox gave them an arrogant smirk. "Has Jack given you the authority to make a sensible deal?" he said.

Tara sat down. Alex sat at her side. Tara reached out. Lennox drew back as if he thought she was going to grab him. She pressed RECORD on the tape deck. The cassettes began to whirl.

"Interview recommenced at twelve thirty-two," Tara said crisply. "The people present in the room are as before."

Lennox glowered at her. "Well?"

"We'll drop all charges except for aiding and abetting a prisoner to escape," Tara said. "That's the best you can get, Chas." She leaned forwards. "Interested?"

Lennox's hand chopped the air. "No way!" he shouted. "If I talk – I walk!"

"We can't do it, Chas," said Alex. "We've got our orders."

"I've got nothing more to say," said Lennox. He stood up, his chair scraping loudly on the floor. "This is over with!"

Tara stared silently up at him with her cold emerald eyes.

"Sit down!" she said sharply.

Lennox sat.

"You have your deal, Mr Lennox," Tara said, the ice in her voice masking her anger. "If you tell us where Stone is, we'll drop all charges."

Lennox grinned. "That's more like it," he said. He leaned back. "Now then, what would you like to know?"

PIC Control.

13:15.

Maddie pressed play on the cassette machine and Chas Lennox's statement began to download into her computer. She didn't like his voice. It was oddly unsettling to her.

But the information he was offering up was hugely significant.

"The original plan was for me to take Mickey straight to Harlow," said the voice. "We were supposed to meet up with some of the guys at the TravelStop Hotel. Know it? Yeah, one of those motorway places. Nothing posh. Unobtrusive, know what I mean? We were going to link up with some of the boys from out of town. Glasgow Jimmy, and Nick the Knife from Birmingham. Major faces from all the big cities. You see, the thing is, word was out that Eddie was going to be there. Yeah – Eddie Stone, large as life." A laugh. "Back from the dead – know what I mean?"

Maddie's ears pricked up at the mention of Eddie. For a while her mind dragged her back to that deadly helicopter ride. That had been the climax of her first case. Something she would never forget.

She shook her head, pushing the images down. But

by the time she managed to get her head clear again, Chas Lennox's statement had moved on from talk of Eddie Stone.

"I'm just hired help," he was saying. "I don't know any of the big stuff. Mr Stone trusts me to do important little jobs for him, know what I mean? I'm good in a tight corner, yeah? I always put up a good fight for Mr Stone. He knows that." The voice droned on.

Maddie let the tape run to its end. It was ironic, the talk of trust – when Lennox was busy selling his boss out to save his own skin. *Honour among thieves,* thought Maddie – *yeah, right!*

She pressed STOP. She moved the mouse and clicked. A screen opened up. It contained a picture of Lennox. Maddie looked at the face and frowned. She gave the file a title. CLENNOXDOC01. She pressed the PLAY icon on-screen to check that the statement had downloaded correctly. Lennox's voice sounded through the speakers.

She paused the file, then replayed it from the beginning.

"...I'm good in a tight corner, yeah? I always put up a good fight for Mr Stone. He knows that."

She frowned. She shortened the section to be repeated and then created a loop. She pressed play.

"...a good fight for Mr Stone – a good fight for Mr Stone – a good fight for Mr Stone..."

Over and over.

Maddie leaned in close to the speakers, her eyes shut tight. There was something about that voice. Something that gave her the creeps. And something about those words. Those particular words – or words very like them.

Where had she heard that voice before?

Where had she heard words like that before?

...a good fight for Mr Stone...

It was maddening, but in the end she had to let it go.

She couldn't get her brain to focus. She could only hope that the answer would eventually come to her of its own accord.

Chapter Eleven

Maddie worked late into the evening. She arrived home light-headed from fatigue. Her gran steered her into the kitchen, sat her down, and put food in front of her. Gran had moved in with Maddie and her father soon after the shooting. She had known they would both need looking after with unobtrusive love and a light touch. No fuss. Just someone there for them to come home to. Someone to hold things together.

Maddie ate mechanically. Grandmother and granddaughter spoke quietly together about ordinary things. Gran's nasturtium out on the balcony, and her battle with the black fly that infested it. The strange noise from the motor of Maddie's Vespa that would need investigating if it persisted. Nothing desperately important – just comforting words to wind the day down.

✪

Harlow, Essex.

North of London.

The TravelStop Hotel, off Junction 7 of the M11.

It was a low-rise sprawl of concrete, glass and steel close to the motorway. A stopover venue for tired salesmen and weary travellers.

The Flamingo Room. A long lounge bar with a sign on the door. PRIVATE FUNCTION. Walls the colour of dried blood. Subdued lighting. A gaggle of small, round tables. On a low stage, a dull-eyed band plodded through a set of familiar songs, fronted by a peroxide skeleton in a black sequinned dress. Cracked make-up and a cracked voice. Wallpaper music that nobody noticed.

Teflon Pat O'Connor was not impressed by the venue. He had flown all the way from Boston, Massachusetts for this? To be serenaded by an ageing hag with a voice like a crow? But he was too classy to make a big deal of it. He wasn't here for the floor show. He was here to meet and greet the big and the bad – to do deals, to avoid unpleasantness and misunderstandings.

At Teflon Pat's table were "friends" from Bristol,

93

Birmingham, Manchester, Newcastle and Glasgow. Big names. Movers and shakers. The criminal aristocracy of Great Britain.

They had all come here under the banner of the Transatlantic Business Symposium. The delegates of the real TBS were dining in another part of the hotel, unaware that gang lords were using their gathering as the perfect cover.

Teflon Pat wanted to carve his own niche into the burgeoning UK gambling industry. The British boys wanted to know what they would get in exchange. Some delicate negotiations were going to be taking place over the next few hours. At Teflon Pat's side was the man who had entered the country under the name Gerald Starkey.

He had spent almost a year undercover in America, getting to know the right people. Patrick O'Connor was the most powerful underworld figure on the Eastern Seaboard. He had spent three months as his house guest – plotting and planning for the day when he could return to London in triumph. And now that day had come and he was making the most of it. He sat at ease beside his powerful partner, holding court as if London was already his.

✪

Maddie fell into bed. She was so tired she could hardly pull the duvet up over herself. A cool, late-evening breeze wafted in through her open windows. Street sounds were carried in. Traffic. Distant voices. And very occasionally a roar, a bellow or a high-pitched call from London Zoo. For Maddie, these were the comforting, familiar sounds of home. She was asleep within moments.

Her mind plunged into a black pit – and at its bottom, a recurring nightmare was waiting for her.

❂

"The key to this whole business," O'Connor's friend said, "is cooperation between our two groups." He smiled around the crowded table. "America and the UK, working together for their mutual advantage." He lifted a full glass. "It's the way to the future, boys."

A man with a face made of granite leaned forwards. Glasgow Jimmy. "That's all very well," he growled. "But what exactly are *you* bringing to the table?"

"London," the man said with a smile. "On a plate!"

There was an uneasy murmur around the table.

Teflon Pat's smooth, cultured voice broke into the groundswell of dissent. "If I'm to take this meeting seriously," he said. "I need to know London is secure. Stonecor has run London for the past few years. My friend here assures me he is in a position to take over its leadership."

"Is that a fact?" snarled Glasgow Jimmy. "And what about Mickey?"

"He's behind bars," said O'Connor's friend. "I'm the new power in London."

There were smiles around the table and more murmurs.

Jimmy grinned. "I've got news for you," he said. "Mickey broke out of Wormwood Scrubs last night. Word is, he's making a comeback."

✪

The nightmare.

The angles of the buildings were all wrong. The road twisted as if it had been wrenched out of shape. The pavement tilted at an odd angle. Everything was in stark black and white. Glaring lights. Sinister black shadows.

Maddie walked through this dark world with her parents at her side. She knew where she was. Outside the stage door of the Royal Opera House. Maddie had danced her heart out that evening. A charity gala performance of *Swan Lake*. Her first performance in front of a paying audience.

They walked arm in arm along the warped pavement. Maddie couldn't stop smiling.

A man stepped out of the shadows.

Lying in her bed, Maddie grimaced in pain. Her head turned on the pillow, her limbs thrashed as she fought to avoid the oncoming horror.

The man had no face. Where his features should have been, there was just blackness.

Gunshots filled the air. Maddie felt her mother falling away from her. Her father threw himself forward to protect her. A roaring pain hit her in the side and sent her spinning. She crashed to the pavement.

A voice spoke from the featureless face. "Goodnight – from Mr Stone." The man turned and melted into the shadows.

Maddie struggled to her feet. She tried to cry out, but she had no voice. She began to run after the fleeing man. She was screaming in pain and terror, but in her nightmare there was no sound – just the endlessness of those familiar, dreadful streets and pavements.

She moaned in her sleep, desperately trying to rip herself out of the nightmare. She never could. It always ran its course.

The man came to bay at the end of a long, narrow alley. She advanced on him, her hands reaching out towards his face. He was wearing a black mask.

She knew what would happen next, it had happened so often, she would tear off the mask and the face underneath would be a white blank. Then she would wake up trembling and sweating.

Her hands tore at the mask.

The mask came away.

She stared.

She came bursting up out of her dream and into sudden wakefulness. She was panting. Her body ran with sweat. The duvet twisted around her. Her eyes opened wide in the darkness.

It had been different this time.

Maddie felt stunned.

She had seen a face.

She had seen the face of the assassin.

○

The man at Pat O'Connor's side took a mouthful of wine.

He couldn't show that he had been wrong-footed by Glasgow Jimmy's news. He had to regroup. Reassess. Come back punching.

"So, Mickey escaped?" he said. "Good for him." He smiled. "I don't think we need worry too much about that old man. He's probably halfway to the Costa by now – he always wanted to retire there." He looked around the table. He lifted his glass. "The old man is dead and gone, boys," he said. "You're looking at the new king."

There was a moment's hesitation around the table.

Then Glasgow Jimmy raised his glass. "To the new king," he said.

Other glasses rose.

"To the new boss of Stonecor."

✪

"Maddie?" Her father's voice from the open doorway of her bedroom.

"I'm OK, Dad."

She sat up. She was still trembling. Her hair stuck to her forehead in wet clumps.

Her father wheeled himself to her bedside.

"Did I wake you up?" she asked.

"No. I was working." He looked at her in the subdued light creeping in from the hallway. "Was it the dream?"

Maddie reached out and took his hand in hers. "Yes," she gasped. His face contracted in sympathy. "But it was different this time, Dad."

"It's only a dream, Maddie," her father said gently.

"No. Please. Listen – you don't understand. It was the voice. I couldn't work it out. I knew I'd heard it before. And those words. They were almost the same. Dad – it was *him*!"

"What voice?" her father asked. "What words?"

Maddie took a long, calming breath.

"The man who killed Mum. The man who shot us." She gripped her father's hand. "Before I passed out, I heard his voice. Remember? I heard him say *Goodnight – from Mr Stone*. And in the dream, when I took the mask off – it was Lennox! It was his voice, Dad! It was Chas Lennox!"

✪

Tara Moon was asleep in an armchair in her spartan North-London studio flat. She had just come to the end of a thirty-hour shift. She was wiped out.

The phone rang shrilly.

She groped for the receiver.

"Tara? It's Jack. Is Lennox still in custody?"

Tara forced her eyes open. "No, sir. He walked early this afternoon."

"Damn!"

Tara sat up. "Problem?"

"Get him back," came the voice down the phone. "I don't care how you do it – I want him back in custody!"

"I'm on to it, sir."

Tara slammed the receiver back into its cradle. She

loped towards the door, grabbing her shoulder bag and jacket as she went. Five minutes later she was behind the wheel of her Golf GTi and heading back to PIC Control. Sleep would have to wait a little longer.

Chapter Twelve

PIC Control.

09:15.

The long, open-plan office was strangely quiet. Alex sat alone at his computer. He was reading the updated Chas Lennox file. The early-morning phone call from Tara Moon had sounded like a bad joke.

"The boss wants Lennox picked up again. It's top priority. I'm pulling you off the Harlow stakeout."

End of conversation.

Alex had learned more once he had arrived at Control. Maddie had made a link between Lennox and the shooting last summer. Alex had absolute faith in Maddie. If she believed Lennox was the gunman, then that was good enough for him. His job was to bring him in.

Alex scrolled through a long section detailing Lennox's past convictions. He moved on to personal stuff. There was an address, but someone had added: *House now empty. No current address on file.* Alex pressed his lips together. That would have been too easy!

There was something about a girlfriend. Alex frowned. The info was ten months old.

There was a picture.

Cherry Low. Twenty-three years old. Bottle-blonde. Fake tan. Big eyes, big lips, big hair.

No other information.

Dead end.

Not necessarily.

Alex opened an Internet link and typed in a website address. The site was password protected. Alex brought up on-screen a list of restricted passwords. He found the one he needed and typed it in. The site opened up for him. A minute later he was looking at Cherry Low's National Insurance file.

He quickly found what he wanted.

She was working at the Hell's Mouth nightclub in Hammersmith.

The file showed her as living at the same address.

In a little flat upstairs, probably, Alex thought.

He closed down the file and snatched his leather jacket off the back of his chair.

Next stop: Hell's Mouth.

✪

Harlow.

A disused factory warehouse with a *Premises To Let* sign outside.

Now PIC Field Control – command centre for Operation Snake Pit.

An unobtrusive van had brought in all the equipment Jack Cooper needed to run a full field operation. The electricity supply had been reconnected. Phone lines had been installed. A TECHSCAN system had been put in place. The outstation unit was linked to four remote cameras, which had been set up on nearby rooftops. The receiver was installed in the warehouse. Maddie was working at the computer that had been designated as the central monitoring station. It was able to receive 4 x 2.1 megapixel digital pictures simultaneously from the C2200 zoom lenses.

All four cameras were focused on the TravelStop Hotel, lying low down beyond a broad area of woodland.

Key info was already coming in.

The hotel had been booked out by an event calling itself the Transatlantic Business Symposium. Behind this grand title was a small group of companies that made cardboard boxes. As far as PIC personnel could find out, the Symposium was an assembly of legitimate business people.

"It's the perfect front," Jack Cooper told Maddie. "Lawful business on the surface, but somewhere, hidden away in the background – a meeting of crooks."

❂

Danny was alone in the MSU, parked up in a quiet lane to the north of the TravelStop Hotel. The back of the white van was a babble of voices – agents sending in reports from all round the perimeter of the hotel. Danny had some sensitive equipment trained on the hotel. The results had been interesting.

There was some hi-tech security stuff in there. Far more than an ordinary motorway hotel would ever need. Someone was making sure that anyone trying to bug the place, either with small location bugs or with long-range listening devices, would only hear white noise.

PIC agents were out there getting visual data. The news was that there were at least twenty security guards patrolling the grounds of the hotel.

"Either the cardboard-box industry has gotten real paranoid recently," Danny murmured to himself, "or I'm staring straight into the snake pit."

Danny opened up his laptop and cracked into the TravelStop Hotel's internal computer network. He scrolled down the list of credit-card bookings, looking for any interesting names. Not that he expected to come up with much. The likes of Glasgow Jimmy Grogan or Nick Ruby, the notorious Birmingham crime lord, were not the kind to leave traces of their movements.

A name took Danny's attention. "Well, look at that," he muttered. "Here's a nasty blast from the past." He stretched out an arm and opened a channel to Field Control.

"Boss? It's Danny. I've just come up with something interesting. You'll never guess who booked in under his own name and paid by credit card."

"I don't have time for guessing games, Danny," Jack Cooper snapped. "Who is it?"

"Patrick Fitzgerald O'Connor of Boston, USA," Danny said. "Large as life."

Maddie knew that name. This was not the first time that Teflon Pat had crossed paths with PIC. O'Connor was on FBI files as being one of the most successful criminals in northeast America. Under a whole string of legitimate companies, it was believed that he had his fingers in criminal activities from New York to Chicago. He was rich, powerful and so far untouchable by any of the US law-enforcement agencies.

"If O'Connor is involved, then this is bigger than we thought," Jack Cooper said to his daughter. His fingers rattled on his desk. "We need someone in there. I have to know what's going on." He flipped a switch. "Danny?"

"Yo."

"Is there any chance that we can monitor what's being said inside the building?"

"No way," came Danny's reply. "First of all, they've got gear in there that would jam our signals, and secondly, they'd detect us the moment we homed in on them. It's too risky, Boss. Sorry."

Maddie interrupted. "Could we send someone in disguised as a member of staff?" she suggested.

Danny's voice wasn't hopeful. "We might just get lucky and sneak someone through their security ring – but they wouldn't be able to carry a wire or any other recording equipment. We'd be sending them in blind. And if anything went wrong, we'd have no way of

107

knowing about it until it was too late."

Jack Cooper shook his head. "It's too high risk for this early on in the game. Keep watching them, Danny – and keep your head down. And that goes for everyone out there – pass the message on. I don't want any mistakes. Everyone is to keep a discreet distance at all times. No one makes a move until I say so. Is that clear?"

"Crystal, Boss," said Danny.

Jack Cooper cut the line.

He looked at Maddie. "And now comes the hard part," he said, his voice a low growl. "Watching and waiting and holding our nerve until we're sure that all the snakes have crawled into the pit – including Mickey and Eddie." He snatched his fist closed. "And then – just when they think they're home free – we take them!"

❂

Maddie stretched her legs. Time was ticking by. Noon had come and gone. Reports came through to Field Control at regular intervals from the agents who ringed the hotel.

"Nothing to report."

"Nothing doing."

"All quiet."

"I'm starving," came Danny's voice into Maddie's headset. "The bad guys are probably in there chugging a seven-course lunch, and I'm down to my last breath mint. Hey, Maddie – any chance of someone bringing me some eatables?"

Maddie smiled. "I'll see what I can do."

Her father was consulting with some Field-Ops Section Heads. Backup strategy – trying to plan for the unexpected.

"Dad?" she called as a lull opened up in the conversation. "Danny's complaining about having nothing to eat. Can I take a break and walk up there with some sandwiches?"

"You're not his waitress," said her father. "Let him get his own food."

"You know he won't leave the van," said Maddie. "It'll only take me half an hour. I could do with the fresh air. It'll wake me up a bit."

Jack Cooper looked at his daughter. What harm could it do? If someone did spot her, all they'd see would be a sixteen-year-old girl taking a walk.

"Go," he said. "And tell Agent Bell that next time he's on duty, he packs his own lunch or he goes hungry."

Maddie found a service station 500 metres away.

She bought some sandwiches and a selection of savoury snacks. A couple of bottles of hi-energy drinks, and a big bag of M&Ms. Danny was an M&M addict.

She knew where to find the MSU. Northwards – on the road that skirted the thick clump of fenced-off woodland between the warehouse and the TravelStop Hotel.

Maddie felt herself waking up a little as she walked along. Two nights of disturbed sleep had drained a lot of energy out of her. It made her brain fuzzy around the edges.

She came to a place where the woodland was less dense. In the far distance, through the trees, she could just make out the shape of the TravelStop Hotel. White walls. Sunlight gleaming on glass. A red roof. She paused, leaning over the fence, staring through the trees. Danny had reported a whole squad of guards patrolling the grounds. She couldn't see anyone.

She climbed the fence and dropped down on to the other side. She paused again, staring through the trees. Nothing moved.

No guards in sight.

PIC were desperate for some idea of what was going on in there.

Maddie guessed that she was about 200 metres

from the building. How risky would it be for her to move in just a little bit closer? To the inner edge of the trees. She might spot something that would be of use to her father.

She slipped light-footed through the trees.

She leaned against a tree trunk. A stretch of open grass lay ahead of her.

She smiled to herself. *Guards? What guards, Danny?*

"Stay right where you are!" The voice came out of nowhere.

Maddie spun round. A man stood behind her. He was wearing a dark blue uniform. He lifted a short black baton and pointed it at her as he strode forwards. "Don't move a muscle!"

She stared at him, unable to think. What should she do? Fight or flee? Either way he'd sound the alarm.

Maddie felt sick.

She'd taken a risk, and she'd lost.

And now, thanks to her, the whole of Operation Snake Pit could be in jeopardy.

Chapter Thirteen

Hammersmith.

Hell's Mouth nightclub.

Alex walked in through the narrow doorway and down a long flight of dingy stairs.

He came to a cramped reception area. A young woman sat behind a counter. Sloppily dressed. Hair wrapped in a scarf. Reading a magazine.

Alex tapped his fingers on the counter top. She looked up at him.

"We're closed," she said.

"I need to talk to a woman called Cherry Low," Alex said.

"That's me." She frowned. "Who are you?"

Alex stared at her in surprise for a moment. Without the hair and the make-up, she looked nothing like her picture.

"I'm looking for Chas Lennox," he said.

"You and me both," said Cherry. "He owes me five hundred quid."

"When did you last see him?" Alex asked.

"Two months ago. Over at the Honey Pot in Charlotte Street – with some dancer called Candy." Her eyes burned with old anger. "She's welcome to him. If you find him, tell him I want my money back."

Alex smiled. "Oh, I'll find him," he said. He turned to leave. He glanced back over his shoulder as he climbed the stairs. "I'll give him your love."

✪

Maddie didn't move. She was hardly even breathing.

The uniformed man walked towards her, swinging his club.

She could not believe that she'd got herself into this position. Two nights of broken sleep, the recurring nightmare, Chas Lennox's voice, memories of Eddie Stone – all these things had messed with her mind so much that she hadn't been thinking straight.

The man came up to her and stood close. Trying to intimidate her.

"What are you doing here?" he asked.

Maddie looked up at him.

Keep cool. Keep calm.

You got yourself into this – get yourself out!

Her mind cleared. Suddenly, she knew what to do.

She pointed over to the building. "Is that the TravelStop Hotel?" she said.

"Yes."

"Great!" She smiled up at the man. "This is my first day here. I thought I knew the way, but I got totally lost." She looked at her watch. "I'm already fifteen minutes late. Can you show me the way to the staff entrance? I'm going to be in so much trouble if I don't report in soon."

The man frowned at her. "You're working here?"

Maddie nodded. "I'm supposed to be," she said. "I'm at sixth-form college. I was told to come here for work experience. And now I'm late, and they're all going to think I'm an idiot."

"What's in the bag?"

Maddie held the plastic carrier bag open for him. "It's my lunch. I'm too nervous to eat it. I really wanted to make a good impression on my first day. I'm going to get such a bad report." She looked anxiously over her shoulder. "Which way is the staff entrance?"

"I'll walk you over there."

It had worked. He had swallowed her nervous-student act.

The walk across the long lawn seemed to take for ever. Maddie's heart was thumping and her legs felt like jelly, but she managed to keep talking. It was vital for her to keep on behaving like an anxious, eager schoolgirl heading for her first-ever job.

The guard led her to a door in the back of the building. There was a sign. STAFF AND DELIVERIES.

She smiled at him. "Thanks," she said. She pushed the door open and walked into the building. The door closed behind her. She leaned against the wall, listening to the blood pounding through her temples.

She had done it. She was in.

She took a deep breath.

She clenched her fist and pumped the air. "Yesss!"

The scary encounter with the guard had shocked her brain into action. The real Maddie Cooper was back... And now she had work to do.

❁

Ten minutes later.

The MSU.

Danny was still waiting for his lunch. Maddie had promised to bring something over. That had been half an hour ago. A guy could starve.

115

Danny's mobile chimed.

He picked it up.

"Danny – it's me."

"Maddie? Where's my food?"

"I'm in the hotel," Maddie said. Her voice was subdued but very excited.

Danny's eyes widened in disbelief. "You went into the hotel to get me some lunch?" he said. "Are you out of your mind?"

"Probably," Maddie said, "but it wasn't like that. Just listen, will you?" She began to explain the situation in a low, urgent voice.

Danny could hardly believe his ears.

"I've found the staff changing room," Maddie continued. "That's where I am right now. If I stop talking, it'll be because someone has come in, OK?"

"Maddie – you've got to get out of there," Danny said.

"I can't," Maddie hissed. "The guard will see me if I try to go back the way I came. That'll blow the whole thing. And if I try to walk out the front way, people are going to want to know who I am."

"Maybe you could get out through a window."

"Oh, right – and that won't look at all suspicious if I'm seen, will it, Danny?"

"I'm going to call the boss, Maddie. We're going to have to send in a snatch squad to get you out of there."

"No! Don't do that," came Maddie's voice. "I'm fine in here, Danny. And I know what to do. I'm going to get myself a waitress's uniform, and I'm going to take a look around the place."

"Maddie! No way!"

"No one is going to pay any attention to one more waitress," Maddie insisted. "I'll just blend in. It'll work. I promise. Dad said he wanted someone in here. Well – I'm in! Listen, just give me time to find out what's going on, and then I'll get out somehow."

"How?" asked Danny.

"I don't know. I'll think of something. Don't tell Dad about any of this just yet. I'll call you."

"Maddie? Don't hang up. When will you call?"

"Soon. Trust me, Danny. It'll be fine. Give me an hour."

"You get back to me within an hour, Maddie," Danny said. "Otherwise, I call the boss! You hear me?"

"I hear you."

The line went dead.

Maddie was on her own in there.

Danny didn't like it.

They hadn't called this Operation Snake Pit for nothing.

Chapter Fourteen

Charlotte Street, London W1.

The Honey Pot.

The sign read: PRIVATE CLUB. MEMBERS ONLY.

The door was closed.

Alex pressed a brass button on the intercom.

"Yes?" rasped a voice.

"Package for a Mr Brown."

There was the click of a lock being released. Alex pushed the door open. A man sat behind a desk. His face creased in sudden suspicion. "Where's the package?" he asked.

"I lied," Alex said. "I'm looking for Chas Lennox."

"I've never heard of the gentleman, sir."

Alex took out his wallet and laid several large bank notes in front of the man.

The money was pocketed in a single, smooth movement.

The man took out a pen and wrote something on a Post-it Note. He slid the note over to Alex.

"I'm very sorry, sir," the man said. "This is a private club. I'm going to have to ask you to leave."

Alex glanced at the piece of paper. It was an address in Chelsea.

"What if I want to join?" Alex asked.

"Membership fees are one thousand pounds per year, sir," the man said. "Payable in advance. We can accept your remittance in cash, or by personal cheque or credit card."

Alex laughed. "I bet you can," he said. He headed for the door.

"Sorry I couldn't be of more help, sir," said the man.

"No problem," Alex said.

The door closed sharply behind him.

He walked over to the side street where he had parked his Ducati.

The search for Lennox was turning into a regular little paper chase.

✪

The TravelStop Hotel.

Staff changing room.

Maddie zipped herself into the black dress. It was a little too short for her and tighter under the arms than she would have liked, but it was the closest fit of any of the spare uniforms she had found in the linen closet. She tied the small lace pinafore around her waist.

She wrapped her own clothes up around her mobile phone and tucked the bundle out of sight at the back of a low shelf. She cracked the door open. There was no one in sight. She slipped out into the corridor. So far, so good.

She could hear the sounds of some major activity further along the corridor. Cooking smells drifted from the same direction.

The plan: find the bad guys. Check them out. Remember faces. See whether Mickey Stone was there. And Eddie. She had to be careful – Eddie Stone knew what she looked like – if he was there she could get into trouble really quickly.

Then she had to get herself and the info out. She still wasn't sure how. She'd worry about that later. When the time came.

She walked to the end of the corridor. To the right she saw a flight of stone steps leading down to a cellar.

To the left, double doors, swinging constantly back and forth as members of staff came and went, carrying plates of food.

Maddie walked quickly towards the swinging doors.

She pushed through into the kitchen. She was hit by a wall of steam and heat. Voices shouting. Stainless steel gleaming. A hundred different smells filling the air. Pots and pans rattling and crashing. Cooks in white. Women in black dresses, men in black trousers and white shirts – moving as if on a conveyor belt.

Maddie found herself in line. A man pushed two plates towards her.

"Table sixteen," he said. The plates were in her hands. She was out of the kitchen, following the line of waiters into a long dining room. There were a lot of people in there – dozens of conversations cutting through piped Muzak. Cutlery clacking. Glasses chinking.

The tables were numbered. She found table sixteen. She off-loaded the plates.

She looked around. There was something wrong with this. At the far end of the room was a sagging banner. ALLIED UK CONTAINERS WELCOMES ITS AMERICAN COLLEAGUES. It wasn't what she had expected. From what she could make out, these were genuine business people.

She remembered her father's words: "*Lawful business on the surface, but somewhere, hidden away in the background – a meeting of crooks.*"

She made her way out of the room. This wasn't where she wanted to be. These people weren't criminals.

Then she noticed a waiter heading further down the corridor. There was another set of double doors. Two big men stood at the doors. They looked like well-groomed thugs.

That was the place.

She went back to the kitchen and picked up another pair of plates.

"Table twenty-three."

The diners at table twenty-three would have to wait. Maddie had other plans. She walked briskly towards the two doormen. Slick young guys in expensive suits. They had hard eyes and big fists.

They let her through.

This room was smaller. Full-length glass doors opened up on to a paved patio with an overspill of tables. A wide, sunlit lawn was bordered by a bank of trees. There were far fewer people here. The voices were louder. There was harsh laughter. The atmosphere of the room was completely different.

A thrill of fear ran through Maddie.

She was in the snake pit.

She recognised some of the faces. People who had only been pictures on computer files suddenly became terrifyingly real. She stood rooted to the spot for a few moments. Her legs wouldn't move.

A frightened sixteen year old in a room full of danger.

Drop the plates and run, Maddie! Get out while you still can!

She ignored the voice that yelled in her head.

No way! I'm here. I stay. I do my job.

She looked around for a table where the occupants weren't eating. She placed the plates in front of two men. They were talking in low voices. They didn't even seem to notice her. That was exactly what she wanted.

She walked over to a long side-table loaded with wine bottles. She picked one up. She wound her way through the tables, topping up glasses. A couple of other waiters moved in and out, pouring wine, taking orders.

She came out into the brilliant sunshine of the patio. There was more laughter. The ring of wine glasses being knocked together. It was all so normal – so

123

ordinary. A group of well-dressed men sat at a table, drinking wine, telling jokes.

A voice called. "Over here, please."

Maddie turned and walked towards the table. An empty glass was being held up towards her.

She glanced around the table. Her stomach tightened. A chill ran through her.

She saw Patrick O'Connor, smiling and laughing at something someone had said. She saw Jimmy Grogan, overlord of the Glasgow underworld. She saw other faces that she knew from PIC files. Powerful men. Bad men.

But it was not any of these who gave her a knot of fear in her stomach.

It was the man who was holding out his empty glass.

His face was turned sideways as he spoke to Pat O'Connor.

It was a face she knew – not from photographs, but from real life.

The face of Eddie Stone.

Chapter Fifteen

The King's Road, Chelsea.

The flat was above an antique shop near the Sloane Square end of the long, lively thoroughfare. Up three flights of stairs. No bell.

Alex knocked on the door.

Nothing.

He hammered again, louder this time.

After a long wait, the door opened a crack. A woman's bleary eyes stared at him.

"I need to speak to Chas," Alex said. "It's important."

"I work nights." The woman sounded sleepy and angry. "You woke me up." She made as if to slam the door shut. Alex jammed his shoe in the gap. She glared at him.

"If Chas is here, I need to see him right now, "Alex said. "If he isn't here, I have to know where he is." He looked steadily at her. "I'm not leaving until you talk to me."

"He's not here," the woman said. "Try Tony's in Great Windmill Street."

"If he's not there, I'm coming right back," he said.

"He'll be there."

Alex removed his foot. The door slammed.

He went back down the stairs. He was beginning to get rattled by this endless run-around. He was talking to too many people – there were too many voices that could whisper in Lennox's ear. *Someone's looking for you, Chas.* If he got a tip-off and went to ground, it might take six months to find him.

Alex had to move fast.

Two minutes later, the silver Ducati was cruising along Eaton Square, heading towards Soho and Great Windmill Street.

✪

The mouth of the wine bottle rattled against Eddie Stone's glass as Maddie poured. Her hands were shaking. Every nerve in her body was screaming for her to drop the bottle and run.

She overfilled the glass. Drops splashed on to the tablecloth, leaving dark red stains.

"Careful," Eddie said, lowering his glass. He gazed at the brimming wine. He smiled. He had still not looked up at Maddie. He lifted his glass. "To full glasses and empty prisons," he said with a laugh. "To good business!"

Maddie backed off. Those ice-blue eyes could turn towards her at any moment. Eddie Stone would recognise her. She had no doubt about that. He would know her in an instant.

She turned and walked quickly off the patio and back into the dining room. She headed straight for the doors, desperate to get out of there before she was discovered. A hole burned between her shoulder blades – the horrible feeling that at any moment a voice would shout, that a hand would catch hold of her, that a pair of deadly blue eyes would pierce her through and through.

She was almost at the doors when something happened that stopped her in her tracks. Something totally unexpected. Something that took everyone in that room unawares.

A noise. Getting gradually louder. A roaring, throbbing, clattering noise, beating in from beyond the open glass patio doors.

127

She turned. Everyone was staring towards the lawn. Midway between the patio and the trees, a blue and white helicopter was settling on to the ground. The downdraught of the rotors flattened a circle of grass. Tablecloths fluttered. A napkin lifted and floated down to the York paving stones.

The engine cut. The rotors slowed and came to a gradual, drooping halt.

The silence was remarkable.

A door opened in the side of the helicopter. A heavy-set, grey-haired man jumped down. He reached up and dragged a younger man out. The second man was a mess. He stooped and shuffled as he was pulled along. His face was bruised. There were flecks of dried blood around his mouth, nose and hairline.

The two men approached the patio, the first man holding the second man's arm in a fierce grip.

Eddie Stone's chair scraped as he stood up. His wine glass fell. It shattered on the ground. He didn't even notice. His face drained of colour.

A wide grin spread across Glasgow Jimmy's face.

"Hello, Mickey. Long time no see."

"Hello, Jimmy." Mickey Stone rested his free hand on Jimmy Grogan's shoulder. Eddie Stone was staring at him. Rigid. Mickey Stone ignored him. He looked across the table at Patrick O'Connor. "Hello Pat."

The American nodded. "That was some entrance, Mickey," he said. "Who's your friend?"

Mickey smiled. "This is Mr Bryson," Mickey Stone said. "He's been planning on giving evidence against all of us in the Old Bailey in a couple of weeks." He locked eyes with O'Connor. "And that includes you, Pat. He knows enough to cause everyone here a lot of trouble."

Bryson looked terrified.

Maddie watched in shocked fascination.

Mickey's eyes swept the table. "He's all yours," he said gruffly. "Do what you like with him. But I have a price." Finally, he looked at Eddie. "I don't know what deals you've been cooking up, son, but you can forget them. I'm back in charge of Stonecor."

"No way!" Eddie's voice was a whisper. He was trembling. "I control Stonecor. You're too late, old man. The deal's been done. You're finished."

Mickey Stone's voice was like iron. "I don't think so," he said.

Eddie threw up his arm, pointing at his father. "You're a dead man," he shouted. "You just don't know when to lie down!" He stared around. The faces turned towards him were expressionless. Eddie looked over his shoulder towards a nearby table.

"Ricky – Blake – show this has-been who's the boss!"

The two young hardmen didn't move.

Maddie saw doubt flicker across Eddie Stone's face.

Jimmy Grogan stood up. He looked at Eddie. "Sorry, lad. It's just business," he said. He rounded the table and shook Mickey Stone by the hand.

"Nice to have you back, Mickey," he said.

Gradually, the table emptied as, one by one, everyone moved towards Mickey Stone.

The last to leave his place was Patrick O'Connor.

He slapped Eddie on the arm. "Nice try," he said. "Maybe another time."

Eddie didn't move. He seemed stunned by the sudden turn of events. Then, in a convulsive movement, he flung the table aside and made a lunge towards his father.

Ricky and Blake were on him in a moment. They drove him to the ground, on to his face, holding his arms, their knees on his back – pinning him down. They looked to Stone Senior for orders.

"Put him somewhere safe," Mickey Stone said. "I'll deal with him later."

Eddie was lifted to his feet.

"Get your hands off me!" he ordered. His voice was wild with anger. The two thugs backed off. Eddie straightened his clothes, dusting his jacket down. He ran his hand through his hair. Regaining control of himself.

Maddie felt a strange kind of sympathy and respect for Eddie Stone. His whole world had been turned inside out in a matter of minutes, but he wasn't finished. He wasn't going to grovel. He was going to fight back.

Eddie looked at his father. His eyes were venomous. "You should be rotting in prison, old man," he whispered. "This isn't over."

"Get him out of my sight," Mickey Stone said. "Put him somewhere to cool off."

Eddie was led away from the patio. Cold eyes watched as he was marched towards the double doors. Eddie's reign had lasted just a few hours. And now he was finished.

Maddie stepped back as the three men approached her.

Eddie's head was held high. He was staring straight ahead, his face devoid of expression.

As Maddie backed off, she bumped against a table. Eddie's eyes flickered towards the sound.

He looked straight into her face.

Maddie's head swam. She felt faint. He had

recognised her. She couldn't breathe.

A light came into his eyes. He smiled.

He stopped and turned, but not towards her. Back towards the room – towards all those loyal friends who had promised him their support.

He began to laugh. He turned again, looking once more at Maddie. Smiling at her. Now she understood the reason for his laughter. He knew that if she was here, then Jack Cooper and the whole strength of PIC couldn't be far behind.

He was smiling because he believed the place was about to be raided.

If he couldn't control Stonecor, then he was happy to see it go down in flames. It was a good joke on his father. And his miserable, treacherous cronies.

The door slammed. He was gone.

Maddie could breathe again. The look on Eddie's face was burned into her mind. That smile. The light that had ignited in his eyes. It was almost as if – it was crazy, Maddie knew it – but it was almost as if he had been *glad* to see her. The thought of it made her head spin.

But she had other priorities. She had to get out of there. Now.

She moved towards the double doors.

A hand caught her arm.

"Just a minute, young lady." She was turned firmly from the doors. She looked into a broad, smirking face. "I'm sorry, but you're not going anywhere."

Chapter Sixteen

A black, top of the range BMW. Driving hard along the M11. Driving north.

Two operatives in the front. Three in the back. The atmosphere in the car was tense – eager. Explosive. All of them were armed.

The man in the front passenger seat had an arrogant face. He was younger than the rest and very much in command. He was hungry for action.

The communications unit bleeped.

"Chaser Two calling. The chopper has come down."

The arrogant young man spoke into the slender microphone. "Where?"

A detailed map reference was given. One of the

operatives in the back had a laptop. He typed in the coordinates and a map appeared on-screen.

"Got it!" he said. "We exit at Junction 7. I'll guide you from there."

The man got busy again with the laptop. "It's some kind of hotel," he said. His fingers rapped the keys. "The TravelStop Hotel."

The younger man spoke. "How long will it take to get everyone in position?"

"Ten minutes," said the laptop man. "Fifteen tops."

The young man nodded. "Perfect. That's all I need to know. Pass the word on to all units – we're going in!" He tapped the driver on the arm. "Move it!"

The motor roared and the car surged along the motorway.

The commander looked over his shoulder. "We've got him, boys," he said. "Mickey Stone is all ours!" He laughed. "It's time to clean up Jack Cooper's mess."

✪

The MSU.

Danny was going out of his mind. It wasn't normal for him to be stressed out like this. When things got hot, Danny usually had ice in his veins. But this was different. Maddie had been out of contact for twenty-seven minutes. Anything could be happening in there.

His hand moved towards the communication console. He had to call Jack Cooper. He couldn't leave it any longer. He hesitated, then withdrew his hand. He had promised Maddie an hour. She still had thirty-three minutes to get back to him.

"Come on, Maddie," he whispered. "Don't do this to me."

A voice broke the tension.

"Agent Hammil to MSU. A chopper just flew over, Danny. I think it came down near the hotel."

Seconds later, half a dozen voices were all reporting the same thing: a helicopter had just come down in the grounds of the hotel. Things were finally happening.

✪

Field Control.

The arrival of the helicopter had created several minutes of frantic action in the abandoned factory. Reports had flooded in from every surveillance point.

The helicopter had flown in from the west. It was a five-seater, turbine-powered Bell JetRanger. Blue and white. A common enough aircraft for someone to rent or borrow – or steal.

It had come down behind a bank of trees – inside the grounds of the hotel.

Tara Moon was at a computer, trying to discover

where it had come from. Communicating with Air Traffic Control. There should be a flight plan. No one seemed able to find it.

A tense silence descended.

Nothing further to report.

The slow minutes ticked by.

Tara looked at her boss. "There's no flight plan," she said. "It's an illegal flight. It has to be Mickey Stone. Do we go in?"

Jack Cooper shook his head. "Not yet," he growled. He slammed his hand down on the arm of his chair. "I have to be certain that Mickey and Eddie are in there."

He stared in silence at the TECHSCAN pictures of the hotel. They told him nothing.

"Maybe we should risk putting someone inside?" Tara said.

Jack Cooper frowned. "They'd never get through the security net. And if they did, they'd have no way of contacting us. Things will have to get a lot worse before I give the order that sends someone into that kind of danger."

A sudden thought struck him.

He looked around.

"Where's Maddie?"

✪

Danny stared at his watch. Ten more minutes, and Maddie would have used up her hour.

It was ten minutes too long for Danny.

"Sorry, Maddie," he said as he reached out and flipped a switch. "I can't handle any more of this." He spoke into the mike of his headset. "MSU to Field Control. I need to talk to the boss."

It was at that moment that Danny's world went crazy.

The MSU rocked wildly. There was a lot of noise outside the back of the van. The doors burst open. Danny was thrown off his seat. He saw two – three – four men come storming into the van. A knee hammered into his chest, nailing him to the floor. A hand tore his headset loose. The muzzle of a gun was thrust in his face.

"Special Branch," shouted the man. "Don't move!"

"I hear you!" Danny yelled, staring at the gun barrel. "I'm not moving!" He tried to suck in some air, but the weight of the man on top of him made it difficult to draw breath. His brain was spinning. This was insane.

"Listen," he gasped, "you've made a mistake, OK? Get my wallet. It's in my pants pocket. Back – right hand side." His voice came in gasps. There were armed men on either side of him.

He was tipped on to his side. His wallet was wrenched out of his pocket.

The man flipped the wallet open. He swore under his breath. "PIC!" he said. "Damn!"

The guns disappeared. Danny was allowed to sit up. He gasped for breath, his chest hurting.

"You're – Special Branch...?" Danny panted. "What – on earth – is going – on?"

"We're after Mickey Stone," said the first man. "We got word he was seen boarding a helicopter out near Luton. We've been monitoring its flight path. It came down near here. We're moving in to arrest him." He gave a sardonic smile. "We're clearing up your boss's mess for him."

Danny stared at him. "You're going in with guns?" he gasped.

The reply dripped sarcasm. "No, we're taking flowers – what do you think?"

Danny's eyes widened in alarm. "We've got an agent in there," he panted. "If you go in like gangbusters, she could get killed! Call it off, for God's sake! Pull your men back!"

The man glanced at his watch. "Too late," he said. "It's already happening."

❂

Field Control.

"Boss? It's Danny." The voice on the speaker was

frantic. "We've got big trouble."

Jack Cooper listened with growing rage as Danny brought him up to speed on the situation. A squad of armed Special Branch officers had gone blundering into the hotel to arrest Mickey Stone. They knew about the criminal summit taking place there. They were banking on some mass arrests. They had no idea that PIC were there ahead of them – they hadn't bothered to check it out.

Jack Cooper pushed his anger aside. Time enough for that later. Right now, he had to deal with the situation that Special Branch had created. And fast.

"OK, Danny," he said, his voice tense. "I'm going to send the troops in. Let's see if we can pull something out of the fire."

"Boss?" Danny's voice was shaking.

"What?"

"Maddie's in there, Boss. She's in the snake pit."

Chapter Seventeen

Great Windmill Street.

Alex walked through to the back of a shop selling London tourist stuff. He pushed a door open. There was a flight of stairs. It led up to the private gambling den known as Tony's.

A huge man with a shaved head stepped out of a side room and blocked Alex's path. He towered over Alex – a wall of stubborn muscle.

"Where do you think you're going, sonny?"

Alex stared up at the man. "Get out of my way," he said, his voice low and menacing. "I'm not in the mood." The hunt for Lennox was beginning to fray Alex's patience.

He made as if to pass the man. A huge hand came out, thudding against his chest.

"Not so fast."

Alex reacted like lightning. The big man didn't know what hit him. It took a split second. Alex snatched hold of his hand and twisted it against the joint. He turned on his heel and executed a perfect hip-throw.

There was a pile-driver noise as the man crashed down on to his back in the hallway. Alex sat on his chest. He had the man's collar in his fist. The man's face was rapidly turning red. He was gasping.

Alex's eyes blazed. "I'm looking for a face called Chas Lennox," he said. "I was told he would be here. Is he?"

The big man shook his head.

"He left – half an hour ago – he went home."

"Home?"

"He's got a gaff near London Bridge."

"What's the address?"

The big man gasped out the information.

Alex knew the place: a rebuilt high-rise block. He could be there in no time on the Ducati.

Alex pulled out his PIC ID card. "If I get there and he's gone," he said, "I'm going to assume you warned him. And if that happens I'm coming back here with a warrant to close this place down. Do I make myself clear?"

The man nodded.

Alex lifted his weight off the man's chest. He helped him to his feet. The man was panting. Winded.

"Sorry about the strong-arm stuff," Alex said, straightening the man's clothes, dusting him down. "You're too big a guy to be doing somersaults. It must have hurt. Are you OK?"

The man stared at him. Breathless. He nodded dumbly.

Alex's forehead wrinkled in apology. "I've had a bad day," he said. "If we met socially, we'd probably get on just fine." He patted the man's shoulder. "Look after yourself."

He walked out through the shop and into the street.

Things were finally looking up.

○

The TravelStop Hotel.

Fifteen minutes earlier.

Jill Ritchie was at the reception desk. Things were quiet. She was reading a magazine under the counter. Sipping from a cup of coffee. Taking a break.

She heard the sudden sound of car wheels spinning on the neat gravel driveway out beyond the front doors. There was a scream of brakes. She looked up. Startled. Half a dozen men came crashing through the doors. They were carrying guns.

Her coffee cup fell. She let out a scream. The men spread out, covering all the exits. One of them ran up to her desk.

"Special Branch," he shouted, thrusting a pass in her face. "Don't panic. Everything's OK."

She stared at the automatic gun in his hand.

Then she fainted.

✪

Things were beginning to calm down in the kitchens. Lunch was over for the day. The staff were clearing away the debris. Chantelle Corday was on the phone, ordering provisions from the wholesaler. As head chef, she always had to be thinking at least two meals ahead.

"And make sure the raspberries are fresh," she said, lifting her voice above the background din of the kitchen. "I had to throw half of them away last time."

The doors burst open. Men came pounding through her kitchen. Armed men. Kitchen staff scattered in panic. There was the clatter of falling pots. The crash of plates. Screams of fear. Someone fell to the floor, tripping someone else. It was chaos. The armed men took no notice.

It was over in a matter of seconds. The swing doors flapped slowly. The men were gone. Chantelle clutched at the telephone, her eyes wide with shock, her chest rising and falling rapidly.

A strange, stunned silence fell over the kitchen. Beyond the swing doors, they could hear thuds and shouts and running feet.

A small voice sounded, unheard, from the telephone. "Is that the end of your order, please? Hello? Hello?"

✪

The Bobby Moore Room.

Lunch was over. Coffee was being served.

Barry Silvester, CEO of Trent, Hatch and McNeil Boxworks plc, was giving a speech.

"I know I speak for all of us in the UK, when I offer a warm welcome to our American colleagues." There was applause. Barry Silvester consulted his notes. "In these days of the Global Economy, it becomes ever more important that—"

There was sudden turmoil at the far end of the room. Every head turned. Barry Silvester stopped in mid-sentence, his mouth open. Men began to pour in through the doors. Men with guns.

They circled the large dining room, facing in towards the stunned audience.

A young man with an arrogant face walked into the room. He strode to the stage. He turned towards the disbelieving throng.

"This is a Special Branch operation," he shouted. "I am Detective Inspector Ian Dowd, and these men are under my command. I want every one of you to assume a face-down position on the floor, with your hands clasped at the back of your heads. I have to warn you that noncompliance with my orders will be met with extreme force."

For a few moments, no one moved. The whole thing was just too grotesque.

"GET ON THE FLOOR!" Dowd yelled. "NOW!"

The stunned diners slid from their seats and stretched out on the floor between the tables. Dowd watched with narrowed, suspicious eyes. The adrenaline was pumping through his system. So far, the operation had gone without a hitch. He scanned the hall – alert for any telltale movement – for any attempt by anyone to reach for a concealed weapon.

He turned. Barry Silvester was still on his feet. He was staring at Dowd in shock.

The young detective inspector took a step towards him. Silvester dropped back into his chair.

"Where's Mickey Stone?" Dowd asked.

Sylvester's mouth opened and closed silently. He was too terrified to speak.

A splinter of doubt entered Dowd's mind. He looked at the other faces at that long table. They all had the same look of subdued panic. He didn't recognise any of them.

He turned back towards the dining room.

Something was very wrong.

Chapter Eighteen

Tara Moon wheeled Jack Cooper along the corridor. A PIC agent opened a door into the Bobby Moore Room. The tables had not been cleared, but the diners were all gone. So were the Special Branch men. Back to their cars and vans – waiting for further orders.

Detective Inspector Dowd sat at one of the tables, his head in his hands.

Tara brought Jack Cooper's wheelchair up to the table.

Dowd looked up. The arrogance was gone from his face.

Jack Cooper stared at him in silence.

Dowd's voice was sullen. "We were acting on good

information, Jack," he said. "No one told me PIC were on the job."

"You gate-crashed an operation that was under my complete control," Jack Cooper said, his voice a low, angry rumble. "You terrorised a hotel full of people. You gave the real criminals time to make a run for it while you put innocent lives at risk. You bungled the whole operation – and you gave Mickey Stone the chance to escape when we had him in the net."

Dowd glared at Jack Cooper. "You can't talk to me like that. I don't answer to you."

Tara winced – expecting an eruption of anger from her boss.

It didn't happen.

Jack Cooper raised his hand. "Tara. Phone."

She handed her mobile to him. He punched out a number.

There was a brief pause while he waited for a reply.

"Jack Cooper here. Could you put me through to the Home Secretary, please."

Detective Inspector Dowd stared at him.

Jack Cooper held the phone out towards Dowd. "Answer to him," he said. He closed Dowd's fingers around the phone. He turned to Tara Moon. "Let's go."

Tara gave Dowd a last look as they headed for the

doors. Her eyes were full of sympathy for the young detective. He glanced up at her. Their eyes locked for a moment, and then he looked away.

He had the look of a man whose high-flying career was about to hit a brick wall.

Tara masked her concern for him as she wheeled Jack Cooper out into the hallway.

Danny came running towards them.

Jack Cooper looked at him. "Well?"

Danny shook his head. He was breathless – his face clouded with anxiety.

"I spoke to a Special Branch man," he said. "He saw someone get into the helicopter just before it took off. He thinks it might have been Mickey Stone. No one's seen Eddie. He might be with him. We don't know."

"I don't give a damn about them," said Cooper. "Where's Maddie?"

"She's still missing," Danny said. "We've looked everywhere. We can't find her." His face showed the guilt that weighed down on him. "They must have taken her with them."

❂

The TravelStop Hotel.

Ten minutes before the Special Branch raid.

Maddie Cooper in a room full of gangsters.

A voice inside Maddie's head was saying: *Stay cool and everything will be fine. If you lose it, the roof's going to come down on you. Just do what they want you to do, and you'll get out of here in one piece.*

They didn't know who she was. They just wanted a waitress – someone to keep on filling their wine glasses while they celebrated the return of Mickey Stone.

The other two waiters had gone before the helicopter had landed. Maddie was in there on her own. She moved from table to table, refilling glasses, keeping her head down – keeping her ears open.

She went out on to the patio. Mickey Stone had taken Eddie's place at the table. Revulsion and anger flooded through her as she looked at him. He was a monster – a smiling, laughing monster.

Richard Bryson sat at his side, his shoulders down, his face haunted and pale. He didn't drink. He just sat there, staring at the tabletop. Ignored by everyone. Waiting for the axe to fall.

Maddie looked across at the helicopter, and then at the bank of trees. She could make a run for it. Get the message out. *He's in here! They're all in here!*

No. There was a better way – a way that would buy her more time.

She went back to the side table. She had been

151

waiting for this: she'd just emptied the last wine bottle.

She looked at the man who stood at the door.

"I need to get some more wine," she said.

Once she was on the other side of that door, she was going to make a dash for her mobile phone. A call for backup. PIC agents would flood into the place. It would all be over.

The doorman walked over to a nearby table and exchanged words with one of the men sitting there. He came back to her.

"I'll go with you," he said. "My boss says to fetch some champagne – plenty of champagne."

Maddie managed not to show her dismay as the man's words shot her plan to pieces.

Adapt to new circumstances.

Improvise.

The man followed her into the corridor.

Now what?

They wanted champagne. Where would she get it from?

She remembered the flight of stairs she had seen earlier – stone stairs leading down to a cellar. A desperate idea came to her.

"This way," she told the man. She headed for the stairs.

They went down into the cellar.

She had to look as if she knew where she was going. She had to lure him to some quiet place where she could put her plan into action. There were storage rooms on either side. She walked past a steel door set in a solid wall. The man laughed. She looked around at him. He jerked a thumb towards the door.

"Eddie's cooling off," he said. "Nice joke."

Maddie frowned. She looked at the door again. It was locked with a heavy steel lever. There was a metal box on the wall. A dial. Some kind of gauge. She suddenly realised what was beyond the steel door. It was a huge commercial freezer.

She understood what the man meant. His callous laughter sickened her.

Eddie Stone was in there.

Cooling off.

20 degrees below zero.

Freezing to death.

Anger boiled up through Maddie. How could anyone behave so barbarically to another human being? Eddie wasn't a good man – but he didn't deserve to die like that. And he wasn't going to – not if she could do anything about it.

She turned suddenly, adopting the *Hachiji-dachi* –

the open-legged jujitsu stance of readiness.

"I'm a police officer," she said. "I want you to lie down on your face with your arms behind your back."

Once he was down, she would tie his hands with the drawstring of her apron. She would secure his feet with his own shoelaces.

The man stared at her for a few seconds, then he burst out laughing. The mocking noise grated in her head.

"I won't warn you again," she said. "Get down on the floor." She hoped she sounded confident. She didn't feel it – she felt very small and very alone.

She remembered her *sensei's* words:

Size does not matter.

Strength does not matter.

Use your whole body to generate power.

The laughter died and the man's face became suddenly hard and vicious. He came at her without warning.

She struck his chest – a straight *Oi tsuki* punch to the sternum. It brought him to a gasping standstill. She spun and delivered a *Mawashi-geri* kick that sent him staggering backwards. A red mist came down over her eyes. She moved in, striking him with her elbow and with her knee. He fell. She came down on top of him.

She struck him twice more before she realised he was no longer moving.

She got to her feet – horrified by the ferocity of her own anger.

The man was unconscious. She stared down at him. She should not have lost control like that. She could have really injured him.

Maddie straightened up. She closed her eyes, standing quite still. Breathing slowly – centring herself. Letting the anger go. Focusing on the task ahead.

She crouched over him, checking him out. He seemed to have been stunned when his head hit the floor. There was a small cut on his scalp – nothing more. She stood up, relieved that he was not seriously hurt.

Maddie needed to be sure that he wouldn't cause her any problems if he woke up in the next few minutes. She untied her apron and bound the cord around his wrists. She unlaced his shoes and tied his ankles.

She turned to the freezer. She stepped up to the steel door and grasped the lever in both hands. She heaved it upwards and heard the sound of the lock disengaging. She pulled the door open. Icy air poured out over her, filling her lungs.

Eddie Stone was curled in a corner, his legs folded up to his chest, his arms wrapped around himself. His hair was frosted, his skin grey – his lips a ghastly blue.

Maddie ran to his side. Her breath fogged. She knelt, taking hold of his bowed shoulders and shaking him. He fell against her. His eyes were closed, his lashes brittle with frost.

Maddie snatched hold of his wrists. She prised his arms loose from his chest. She stood up, bent her back and dragged him along the floor. He was a dead weight. His skin was horribly cold. She hauled him out into the corridor, then slammed the freezer door, cutting off the flow of icy air.

Maddie fell to her knees.

Eddie didn't seem to be breathing.

Her fingers trembled as she felt for a pulse.

There was nothing.

His blood pressure was at zero.

She shook him. She brought her mouth up close to his ear.

"Eddie! You're OK, now!"

Nothing.

She struggled to remember her CPR training: cardiopulmonary resuscitation. How to save a life.

She knelt at his head. She slid a hand under his neck, tilting his head back. His mouth came open. She leaned over him, closing his nose off with her finger and thumb. She pressed her open mouth against his. She breathed into his mouth. His chest rose. She pulled away. His chest fell. She breathed into his mouth again, counting out two seconds in her head, filling his lungs.

"Breathe!" she gasped. "Eddie! Please! Breathe!"

There was no response from him.

She moved down to chest level. She laced her fingers together. She pressed her palms down into the centre of his chest. She began to pump. She compressed his chest fifteen times.

She went back to his head, locking her mouth against his, giving him two two-second breaths. She lifted her head. A choking noise came from his open mouth. His chest rose and fell as he fought to breathe.

She sat back on her heels. Her heart was racing. She found she was holding his cold hand between hers, chafing it for warmth.

"Come on, Eddie," she murmured.

His eyelids flickered.

His blue eyes swam.

"Eddie?"

His head turned towards the sound of her voice. "Cold..." It was only a whisper.

"We have to get out of here. They'll come looking for me. Can you walk?"

157

"I don't know."

"I'll help you." She stood up. She bent over, hooking her fingers under his arms. With painful slowness, she managed to get him to his feet. He rested his arm across her shoulders, leaning his whole weight on her.

She stared around searchingly. She needed to take him somewhere where he could recover – if only for a few minutes.

She guided him towards a door. She opened it and they both stumbled inside. It was a linen closet. She sat him on a large wicker basket, and put her arms around him to stop him from toppling to the floor. His head lolled against her. She felt the warmth being leached out of her. She felt his coldness creeping into her.

She looked down at his bowed head. She could still feel the icy imprint of his lips on hers. She closed her eyes as the full impact of what she had just done hit her like an express train. She had saved Eddie Stone's life. Without hesitation – without a moment's thought – she had saved the son of the man who had ordered her mother's murder.

Things didn't get much more real than this.

✪

It was at this same moment that Special Branch raided the hotel above Maddie's head.

Armed officers took out the perimeter guards. Cars screeched to a halt in the driveway. Detective Inspector Ian Dowd led his men into the reception lobby. Marksmen covered every entrance and exit – they poured through the building – determined to secure the entire site in one massive strike.

In a quiet lane to the north of the hotel, four Special Branch officers stormed the MSU, pinning Danny to the floor and holding a gun to his head.

Armed men in flak jackets flooded across the lawn towards the helicopter.

The pilot started the engine. The rotors began to sweep.

Panic erupted on the patio and in the room beyond. People were running in all directions, shouting, knocking tables over – desperate to escape.

Only one man kept his cool. Mickey Stone ran straight for the helicopter, moving quickly despite his bulk. It was a police raid. He had to get out. He heaved himself up inside the helicopter and slammed the door. The aircraft lifted off, skimming the heads of the invaders – throwing them on to their faces in the grass.

Mickey Stone stared down out of the glass door-panel as the helicopter rose into the air.

A single figure stood unmoving in all the chaos. Pat

O'Connor still had his wine glass in his hand. He looked up towards the helicopter.

Mickey saw Pat raise his glass towards the aircraft – as if making a toast.

Mickey smiled.

Grace under fire. It would have been a great partnership.

The last thing Mickey Stone saw before the helicopter turned and sped away over the treetops, was O'Connor taking a drink from his glass as the armed police officers moved in on him.

Chapter Nineteen

Eddie's hand reached up and his fingers touched Maddie's cheek. His voice was soft and low. Filled with amazement.

"You saved my life," he said. "After everything my family has done to you."

Maddie looked into his eyes. His fingers were cold on her skin. She was terribly aware of his touch.

"I couldn't just let you die," she said. Her mouth was dry.

Eddie lifted himself slightly, his hand still cradling her cheek.

"I've thought about you so much, Maddie," he whispered. "Remembering. Regretting what happened.

Wishing things had been different."

Maddie's voice was calm and steady as she replied. "You were going to kill me." She struggled to keep that idea clear in her head. "Yes. I think you were."

He looked up at her. "No. I would never have harmed you." He winced, as if hit by bad memories. "I was desperate. I wasn't thinking straight," he said. "I panicked. That's not who I am, Maddie. Not deep down. That's my father – not me."

She shut her eyes tightly. Trying not to listen.

"I can only guess at how terrible the last year has been for you, Maddie," Eddie said gently. "All your wishes and hopes and dreams – torn apart by that evil man."

Maddie's voice was only a whisper. "He's your father."

"He was never a normal father to me," Eddie said. "I hate him."

He sat up. Maddie opened her eyes. His face was very close to hers. She found that she couldn't look away. He was still shaking, and his face was deathly pale, but she could see that his strength was slowly returning.

"I would give anything for that terrible thing never to have happened," he said.

Her heart hardened for a moment. "Would you?" she said, pushing his hand away from her face. "What would you give, Eddie? Tell me. I'd really like to know."

His head drooped. "I'm sorry," he said softly. "I deserved that." His eyes were on her again. "I know it doesn't help, but I do understand some of what you must have gone through, Maddie. My mother died when I was sixteen."

Maddie stared at him. She remembered from the files that Mickey Stone was a widower – but she had never related it to Eddie before.

"She died of cancer," Eddie said. "It's just as brutal, in its way. Except that it takes longer. I had to watch my mother withering away in front of me. You don't get over a loss like that, do you?"

Her voice was a breath. "No. You don't."

Eddie straightened up. "I want to make a difference, Maddie," he said. "I want to pull Stonecor away from all the illegal businesses. I want to make it legitimate. That's why I was so desperate to get control of it." He looked into her eyes. "I nearly beat Mickey today, Maddie. I nearly defeated him." His voice cracked. "Now he wants me dead."

Maddie swallowed, shocked by the fear in his voice. "There are PIC agents all around the building," she said. "You'll be safe once we get through to them."

Eddie stared at her. "I'm a wanted man. I'll go to

prison. And one night, my father's people will come for me and in the morning I'll be found with my throat cut." His eyes were pleading. "I was forced to work for my father," he said. "I was never given any other choice. You can't let them kill me, Maddie."

He put his hands on her shoulders but she pulled herself away. "You can't expect me to let you walk out of here," she said desperately. "I can't do that."

Eddie sat up, his compelling eyes on Maddie's face. "Your people don't have much real information about Stonecor, do they?" he said. "That's because the bulk of the paperwork is abroad. In Paris. I can get that information for you. I can give you everything you need to close Stonecor down once and for all. Listen to me, Maddie, I'm not asking you to let me walk away. Come to Paris with me and I'll give you the details of every crooked deal my father has ever made."

There was a long silence.

"I can't go to Paris with you," Maddie said at length. "You have to talk to my father – tell him everything you've told me." She looked into his eyes. "He'll listen – I promise he will."

Eddie lowered his head. "If that's your best offer, I'll take it," he said. "I trust you, Maddie – you know that, don't you?"

She ignored the question. "Can you walk yet?" she asked.

He stood up and stamped his feet. He smiled and nodded.

"We need to get out of here," she said.

"I'm completely in your hands, Maddie."

She frowned at him.

They walked towards the stone stairs. The man was still lying unconscious beside the freezer. Maddie was suddenly aware of a lot of noise coming from above. She gestured for Eddie to wait. Stealthily, she climbed the stairs.

She saw a couple of uniformed men. Running. They had police-issue bulletproof vests. They were carrying guns. She kept herself well back. She didn't recognise the men. They weren't PIC agents.

Her brain raced. The hotel had been overrun by police officers – but not by members of PIC. Who, then? The Flying Squad? Possibly. Special Branch? Yes, probably. She remembered that they had offered to help with the search for Mickey Stone. Maybe they hadn't taken no for an answer.

Her father would never have called in Special Branch – not when he had his own agents on site. They must be acting independently. Anger flared through her. She wouldn't let Special Branch capture Eddie. Her father had worked too hard for his prize to be snatched away like that.

She crept back down to where Eddie was waiting.

"There's a police raid going on," she told him. "But it's not my squad. They're armed. If we show ourselves, they'll arrest you. We have to get through to my father."

He closed his fingers around her wrist. "We'll get out, Maddie," he said. "I know we will."

She looked at him. That was more than she knew.

✖

Slowly, and with difficulty, Maddie and Eddie Stone managed to make their way undetected to the main reception area. There were guards on the doors. Maddie couldn't think how to get past them. She watched the armed police officers from where she was hidden, behind the temporarily deserted reception desk. Lost for ideas. They knew they would be discovered at any moment. Time was running out.

Eddie tapped her arm. He pointed. She nodded. They slipped into an office, keeping low. Eddie crawled over to a large pin board. Car keys hung from pegs. The TravelStop Hotel had valet parking.

Maddie kept watch while Eddie reached up and snatched a key from the board.

They crawled to the window. It was a hot day. The window was open.

A few silent seconds later and the two of them were out of the building, pressed against the wall, waiting for their chance to slip away towards the car park.

Eddie led the way at a crouch. Maddie was right on his heels.

Eddie pointed the remote tag towards the cars. He pressed a button. Lights flashed three times on a blue BMW Roadster.

Moments later they were beside the high-performance sports car. Eddie opened the driver's door. He slid inside. Maddie circled the car and got in on the passenger side. They were both breathing fast. The blood was pounding through Maddie's head so hard she could hardly think.

"We'll only get one chance at this," Eddie said as he slipped the key into the ignition. "Hold tight, Maddie. This could get a bit wild."

He turned the key. The car leapt forwards in a spume of gravel. They were halfway to the main gate before she saw anyone. Guards. At the gates. Armed. Turning. Staring. Shouting. Pointing their weapons.

Eddie put his foot down. The Roadster shot forwards like a bullet. Two security men flung themselves aside

167

as the sleek car bolted through the gates. Eddie spun the wheel. Rubber burned as the back of the car swung round. For a moment she was afraid that he'd lose control. But he spun the wheel the other way. The car righted itself. The force thrust Maddie back into the leather seat. They sped down the road. The wind whipped her hair about her face.

"Eddie – slow down. We have to turn off soon – we have to get to Field Control."

Eddie's voice was calm. "I'm sorry, Maddie," he said. "I really don't think that's such a good idea after all." He glanced at her, his eyes shining. "We don't need your dad, Maddie. We'll do just fine on our own."

Chapter Twenty

The TravelStop Hotel.

Richard Bryson stood between two PIC agents. He was pale. His expression was a mixture of relief and resentment.

"You were supposed to be protecting me," he said. "Stone took me from right under your noses. I could have been killed."

Jack Cooper looked up at him. "If you had chosen at the beginning to tell us everything you know, Mr Bryson," he said, his voice deep and slow, "you could already be living in complete safety with a new face and identity."

Bryson's voice was scornful. "I told you the deal. I

get the face and the ID before I tell you a thing. And I won't do it until Mickey Stone and that crazy son of his are behind bars." His eyes flared. "Where's Mickey now? He got away, didn't he?"

"Mickey Stone won't get near you again," Jack Cooper said. "I can promise you that."

"You can't stop him," Bryson shouted. "You can't protect me from him."

Jack Cooper looked at his agents. "Take care of him," he instructed. "Clean him up and put him somewhere safe."

Bryson was taken to a waiting van.

Jack Cooper looked up at Tara. "Now what?"

"O'Connor," she replied. "He's in the manager's office."

"Can we hold him on anything?" Jack Cooper asked.

"Only if there's a law against wearing Armani suits," Tara said.

Jack Cooper frowned. "Let's get it over with."

Tara wheeled him to the manager's office.

Patrick O'Connor was behind the desk, leaning back in the hotel manager's chair and talking on the phone. He glanced at Jack Cooper. He gave a small nod of acknowledgement, talking all the while.

"Thank you, Branford. No, I don't think we're going to have any problems here. But keep your team on standby just in case. I'll be in touch." He put the phone down. He turned to Jack Cooper. "That was my lawyer," he explained. "But we won't be needing lawyers, will we?" He smiled. "You would be Detective Chief Superintendent Cooper, I presume?" He leaned across the desk and held out his hand. "It's a pleasure to meet you."

Cooper shook the offered hand.

"I don't know whether you realise it, Jack," said O'Connor. "I can call you Jack, can't I?" Cooper gave a curt nod.

"Jack, you have done me an enormous favour." O'Connor spread his hands. "I was planning on doing business with those people," he said. "I came all the way from Boston – in good faith – to set up some trade agreements." He smiled wryly. "Can you imagine my embarrassment when I learned that they were nothing but a bunch of criminals?"

Jack Cooper looked steadily at him. "A man in your position should be a little more careful who he has dealings with," he said.

"I totally agree with you," O'Connor replied. "It could have done irreparable damage to my reputation in America."

There was a pause. The two men fenced with their eyes. Neither looked away.

 171

"I am well aware of your reputation in America, Mr O'Connor," Jack Cooper said coldly. "I've seen your FBI files."

O'Connor was still smiling, but his eyes were like flint. "Then you will also know that I'm a major investor in the Boston Container Company, and that I flew to the UK in order to attend the Transatlantic Business Symposium." He spread his hands. "Check the records, DCS Cooper – I booked into this place under my own name and I paid with my own credit card. What kind of a person would do that if they were planning on meeting up with a bunch of crooks?"

"A clever person might," Jack Cooper said. "If he thought there was a risk of something going wrong. If he wanted to be able to say he had a legitimate reason for being here."

O'Connor's smile faded. He pushed back the cuff of his cashmere Armani jacket and looked at his Rolex. A white gold Oyster Cosmograph Daytona with a black leather strap. "Are we finished here?" he asked. "Can I help you in any other way?" It was a dismissal. Jack Cooper bit back his irritation.

"Will you be leaving the country now, Mr O'Connor?"

"On the first available flight."

"Have a safe journey," Jack Cooper said as he

turned his wheelchair to leave the room. "And be careful, Mr O'Connor. Be very careful." His words were barbed.

"Oh I am," O'Connor said with a laugh. "I always am."

Tara knew how much that meeting must have rankled with her boss. But right then, Jack Cooper had far more urgent things on his mind. The MSU was parked at the front of the hotel. Danny was coordinating efforts to track the helicopter.

The back doors of the van were open. Danny was in there, hunched over his equipment.

He heard the sound of Jack Cooper's wheelchair on the gravel. He looked up. Jack Cooper didn't need to ask for an update – the expression on Danny's face said it all.

Maddie was still missing.

❁

The BMW Roadster was speeding south along the M11, heading for London.

"You have to let me contact my father," Maddie insisted. "We have to go back."

Eddie frowned. "I can't risk it, Maddie," he said. "I'm sorry. I don't have any reason to believe your father will help me."

173

"I'm helping you, aren't I?" said Maddie.

Eddie flicked a glance at her. "That's different," he said. "We have a special bond."

Maddie didn't like the sound of that. "No," she said. "We don't."

"You saved my life back there, Maddie."

"I'd have done that for anyone."

"But you did it for me." Eddie smiled. "You're an amazing person, Madeleine Cooper. Do you know that?"

Maddie didn't respond.

There was silence between them for a while. Maddie knew that she needed to take control of the situation, but until they came off the motorway, or until Eddie was prepared to pull over, there wasn't much she could do.

"Do you trust me, Maddie?" he asked suddenly.

She stared at him. "No."

A flash of disappointment came over his face. "That's a pity," he said. "I'd trust you with my life." He glanced at her. "Listen, Maddie – if I wanted to hurt you, then you'd already be hurt. If I wanted to get away from you, I'd dump you at the roadside."

She kept her voice unemotional – detached. "Your point being?"

His face grew desperate. "I'm drowning here, Maddie. I need your help."

She could feel herself melting towards him. "I will help you," she said. "But not to run away like this. It's not right, Eddie. This isn't the way to do things."

"I'm not running away, Maddie," he said. "This is a temporary retreat, that's all. Listen – you have to trust me to get the information I told you about. Then, I can do a deal that will keep me out of prison. I'll turn everything over to the police if they agree to drop all their charges against me. That's fair, isn't it?"

"I can't make that decision," Maddie said firmly.

"Give it some more thought, Maddie – at least until we hit London," Eddie said. "If by then, you still think you should turn me in – so be it. I won't stop you." He glanced at her. "Do we have a deal?"

"I suppose so," she answered uneasily. "Yes. OK."

He smiled. "I know you'll make the right decision, Maddie," he said.

She looked at him. She wished she felt so sure.

Chapter Twenty◦one

The M11.

Theydon Bois. The M25 intersection.

Tara was driving the Golf GTi. Danny was at her side.

They were in the outside lane – cruising past the other traffic as if it were standing still.

They were following a lead.

A blue BMW Roadster had broken out of the hotel. Reports from Special Branch stated that there was a male at the wheel, and a young female passenger. Danny had managed to get access to some CCTV Roadwatch footage. He had pinpointed the Roadster as it had joined the A414 at Church Langley – heading for the motorway. He had computer-enhanced the still shots. Blown them up on-screen. They were blurry, but the faces were recognisable.

Eddie Stone – and Maddie.

Jack Cooper had sent Danny and Tara in pursuit.

The Met were given a description of the stolen car and its occupants. Jack Cooper's orders were to put a close tail on the car – but not to intercept it.

The car was being driven by a ruthless and dangerous man – and he had a hostage. Maddie's safety had to be the number-one priority.

Tara drove with calm self-assurance. It was only when Danny glanced at the speedometer that he realised just how fast they were going.

He looked questioningly at her.

"Problem?" she asked.

"Did you know there was a speed limit in this country?" he asked.

"Yes. Why?"

"Oh – no reason. I was just making conversation."

A voice on the intercom: *"Target vehicle has turned on to the North Circular Road at Junction 4. Now heading west."*

A satellite navigation console was fitted to the passenger-side dashboard. Danny punched in some details. A map of North London zoomed in.

"They're about ten kilometres ahead of us," he told Tara. "If they stay on the North Circular, it'll take them through Epping Forest and on to Edmonton."

Tara shook her head. "I don't think so," she said. "My guess is Walthamstow – and then down into Central London. Eddie will have friends there – places to lie low and plan his next move." She put her foot down and the car rocketed forwards.

Danny looked at her in alarm.

"We need to make up some time," she told him. "Trust me, Danny – I know what I'm doing. I got top marks on the Advanced Driving Course at Hendon."

Danny decided to concentrate on the SatNav console. He preferred not to watch the motorway bridges whipping past.

Another call came through only a couple of minutes later.

"*Suspect car has turned south on to the A112.*"

Danny looked at the map. He smiled as he saw where this was leading.

Walthamstow.

✪

Helen's Café, Walthamstow.

The walls were tiled white. There was a long, stainless steel counter. Bacon and eggs sizzled on hotplates. Chips bubbled in oil. Tea brewed in a stainless steel urn. Order slips hung from bulldog clips behind the counter.

The place was noisy and busy.

The tabletops were Formica. The chairs had plastic covers.

Maddie and Eddie sat facing one another at a window table.

Eddie was sipping black coffee. Maddie's drink stood untasted. Eddie's mobile phone lay on the table between them.

Maddie stared at it.

Up until then, she hadn't even known he was carrying a phone.

Eddie watched her carefully.

Maddie was torn with uncertainty. Part of her wanted to believe Eddie, but a voice in her head warned her of the danger that lay ahead if she didn't stop this right now.

But was she in danger?

Could she trust him?

"To call, or not to call," Eddie said, breaking a five-minute silence. "It's up to you, Maddie." He gestured towards the phone. "I'm trusting you to make the right decision."

She frowned. "Stop saying that," she said quietly. "It doesn't make any difference whether you trust me or not."

He held his hands out in a gesture of quiet surrender. "All you have to do is to pick up the phone and call your father," he said. "Make the call, if you think it's the right thing to do. Everyone else has betrayed me – why shouldn't you? I won't try to get away." He tapped the tabletop with his index finger. "But if you decide to do that, Maddie, I won't be handing over the Stonecor files."

She looked at him.

"They'll send me to prison, Maddie. If that happens, I'm a dead man. Why should I hand them Stonecor on a plate?" His eyes burned. "On the other hand, you could let me make a call. I know a guy – he'll fix all the arrangements for us to travel to Paris. We could be there by the end of the day, Maddie. And by tomorrow, your father will have all the information he needs – right on his desk. And that's a promise." He gazed steadily at her. "It's all a matter of trust, Maddie. In the end, everything comes down to trust. Trust earns rewards."

She looked at him. She felt torn apart.

What was the right thing to do?

She lowered her eyes to the mobile phone. "Make your call," she said.

✪

Tara swore under her breath as she brought the car to a stop. They were at a crossroads. The traffic lights were red.

She looked at Danny. "Any ideas?" she said.

Danny shook his head. There had been no further reports of the Roadster since it had turned south into Chingford Road. Danny stared down at the network of roads that filled the screen of the SatNav console. Unless there was a new sighting, they might as well flip a coin to choose a route.

The lights turned green.

The traffic began to move.

Tara kept on the straight road south.

They passed Helen's Café. They didn't see the BMW Roadster tucked away in a side street. They drove past it at the very moment Eddie Stone picked up his phone and began to dial.

✪

An apartment block near London Bridge.

A window with a Venetian blind.

A kitchen.

Chas Lennox was grilling bacon. Two thick slices of

bread lay waiting. There was a large bottle of tomato ketchup and a can of lager beside the bread.

Chas took a swig of lager and prodded the bacon with a fork.

His mobile phone rang.

He flipped it open one-handed.

"Lennox."

A voice spoke in Chas's ear. His face registered complete surprise. "Eddie? Where are you?"

The bacon spat grease. Chas turned the heat down.

"Yes, I'm listening," he said. "Don't worry, Eddie – just tell me what you want and I'll sort it for you." He strode across the kitchen. He found a pen. He turned a newspaper over and started to scribble instructions in the margins.

The call was brief. Chas pocketed his phone. He began to laugh.

He returned to the grill and switched off the gas, then lifted his jacket off the back of a chair and left the room.

Chas went down to the street and got into his car. As he drove off, he took his mobile out again and dialled a number. He heard the ringing tone at the other end.

"Yes?"

"It's Chas. I've got some interesting information for

you, Boss." He began to laugh again. "You're never going to believe who I just got a call from."

✪

Alex rode his motorbike along Upper Thames Street. The long grey span of London Bridge rose up ahead of him. He took a left. Keeping his eyes open. Looking for a specific address.

He turned a corner and began to drive slowly along the street. There it was. A newly refurbished high-rise apartment block. He drove past and parked the Ducati a little further along the street.

Alex climbed off the bike. He took off his helmet and smoothed his hair. He looked up towards a window. It was a good guess. The window had a Venetian blind.

Behind the blind, four strips of bacon were withering in a grill pan.

Alex had missed Lennox by seven minutes.

Chapter Twenty•two

Prince Albert Road, NW1.

Maddie's home.

Maddie ran up the communal stairs three at a time, her face pale and anxious. She had to act fast. She had left Eddie at the wheel of the Roadster. It was parked outside the front entrance of the building – its engine running.

But would he still be waiting there when she came back down?

It was a risk she had to take. Part of her almost wished he would make a break for it. At least that would save her from the uncertainty that was tormenting her.

She pulled out her door key as she came to her own floor. She was panting as she fumbled at the lock of her front door.

The door opened from the inside.

"Hello, Maddie. You're home early."

Maddie stared at her gran. She had hoped the flat would be empty.

Jane Cooper frowned as she saw the state that her granddaughter was in. "Is something wrong?" she asked.

"No. It's nothing, Gran," said Maddie. "I forgot something – for work – I have to get it."

She ran in past her gran, her face burning. She had to act fast – to be in and out before her gran had time to ask any questions. Maddie was a bad liar and her gran was far too sharp-witted to be fooled by evasive answers.

Maddie burst into her bedroom. She dived across the bed and threw open the door of her bedside cupboard. She scrabbled through old magazines and letters and wads of photographs. It had to be there somewhere.

Groaning with frustration, she heaved the contents of the cupboard out on to the floor. There it was! She lifted her passport out of the mess and thrust it into her pocket.

She ran for the door. As she passed her desk, she picked up a Manila envelope.

Her gran was still standing at the open front door. Maddie waved the envelope at her as she ran past. "Got it!" she said, forcing a smile. "I'd forget my head if it wasn't screwed on, wouldn't I, Gran."

The old lady didn't respond to the weak joke. "Is everything all right?" she asked, reaching out a hand to Maddie.

"Of course!" Maddie said. She paused and gave her gran a quick kiss on the cheek. "I have to go."

"You be careful," her gran called after her as Maddie went bounding down the stairs.

"I will!" Maddie shouted back.

She dropped the envelope.

She ran through the foyer and out into the street – half-convinced that the Roadster would be gone.

It was still there. Eddie was still at the wheel.

Maddie climbed in, breathless – hot and sweaty from her exertions.

He looked at her. "Are we beginning to trust each other yet, Maddie?" he asked, smiling.

She looked at him. She didn't reply.

He laughed as he gunned the engine.

The Roadster sped off.

Leyton, North London.

Near the A102 Cross Route.

Tara had drawn in to the kerb. It made no sense to drive aimlessly through the tangle of North London streets. Until they got some fresh information about the target car, they weren't going anywhere.

Tara's nails rattled on the steering wheel.

Danny stared at the SatNav screen.

Where was that Roadster?

It couldn't have just vanished. It had to be somewhere.

A voice crackled on the intercom.

"A car answering the description of the stolen vehicle has been seen parked at Euston Station."

"Yesss!" Tara kicked the car into gear.

They were back on the road.

○

Euston Station, NW1.

The station colonnade.

"There it is!" Danny pointed. "Look!"

Tara brought them to a halt behind the Roadster.

They both got out. They approached the car – Danny on one side, Tara on the other.

"Nice car," she said. "2.5 litre dual overhead cam, 24 valve, 6 cylinder engine. Beautiful."

"Eddie Stone only steals the best," said Danny.

They looked at one another across the low bonnet of the car.

Tara rested the flat of her hand on the shining blue metal. "The engine's cold," she said. "They've been gone a while."

Danny stared towards the station.

"Do you think they caught a train?" he asked.

Tara shook her head. "Not overground. That would take them north: to the West Midlands and along the west coast. Eddie wouldn't have driven all the way down here just to catch a train to take him back the way he'd come."

"What about the Underground?" Danny suggested. "Euston is a crossover for the Northern Line and the Victoria Line."

Tara looked at him. "OK – I'll take the Northern Line," she said dryly. "Do you want to look for them on the Victoria Line? They shouldn't be too hard to find. How many people use the London Underground every day? Two and a half million?"

Danny frowned. "Point taken," he said. He slammed his hand down on the roof of the Roadster. "Damn!" He looked at Tara. "Do you want to tell the boss that we've lost them again?"

Tara shook her head. But it had to be done. She walked back to their car.

Danny stared in anguish at the station building.

"Maddie? What's going on?" he murmured under his breath. "Why don't you cut loose from him? Where is he taking you?"

Chapter Twenty-three

Waterloo Station.

It had been Eddie's idea to leave the car at Euston and travel the seven stops south on the Underground.

Maddie walked along at Eddie's side in pensive silence. She thought she had made her decision. She would go with him to Paris on the express train. She had picked up her passport. She had made up her mind – except it was still pulling in two different directions. The more she tried to convince herself that she was doing the right thing, the more she doubted it.

She glanced at him. What was really going on behind those ice-blue eyes?

Trust him. Don't trust him.

Go with him. Don't go with him.

The situation was tearing her apart.

They walked past a flower stall. Eddie paused.

"Hello, Spike," he said.

A grey-haired man stepped from behind a bank of cut flowers. "Eddie!" he said, smiling broadly. "I thought you'd left town!"

The two men embraced.

"I came back," Eddie said. "It's good to see you, Spike."

Spike looked at him. "Do you need any help?" he asked. "Is there anything I can do?"

Eddie smiled. "Everything's under control," he said.

"If you're sure," said Spike. "I still owe you, don't forget."

Eddie raised a hand. "It was nothing." He turned towards Maddie. "But if you're feeling generous, I'll take a rose for my friend."

"Take a bunch, Eddie," Spike said, smiling at Maddie. "Take two bunches!"

"No. One perfect rose will do."

Spike pulled a red rose from a bunch in front of the stall. He handed it to Eddie.

Eddie held the stem between his fingers. He lifted it to his face and breathed in, smiling.

Then he held it out towards Maddie.

She stared at him.

"Take it," he said.

"Why are you doing this?" Maddie asked.

"It's a rose for a beautiful English rose," he said. "A gift. That's all."

Confused, Maddie reached for the flower.

A thorn pierced her finger. She drew her hand back from the sudden sharp sting. Eddie caught her wrist. There was a small bead of blood. Eddie lifted her hand to his mouth and kissed the blood away. Maddie looked into his face and saw that his eyes were fixed on hers.

The hair stood up on the back of her neck.

She pulled her hand away.

Neither of them spoke.

Eddie dropped the rose to the ground. He lifted a foot and brought his shoe down on the flower. He twisted his heel, grinding the petals to a dark red mush.

She stared at him, startled by the anger that darkened his face as he destroyed the flower.

He smiled at her, his face calm again.

"I won't have you hurt, Maddie," he said softly. "You mean too much to me."

✪

They walked through the main concourse of Waterloo Station.

"What did that man at the flower stall mean when he said he owed you?" Maddie asked Eddie.

"I did him a small favour once, that's all," Eddie said. "Some people were bothering him. I convinced them to leave him alone." He looked at her. "It's what friends do. They help each other. Just like we're helping each other."

Maddie frowned. "We're not friends, Eddie," she said.

"No?" He sounded hurt. "That's a shame."

They came to the head of the stairs.

Eddie pointed towards a café. Bonapartes. There were potted plants and wooden tables on the forecourt. "Can I buy you a coffee?" he said. "Even though we're not friends?" He walked towards the café without waiting for a response.

Most of the tables were occupied. Eddie found an empty one. He sat down. Maddie stood looking at him. He gestured towards a chair. She sat.

"What's going on?" she asked.

"I'm ordering coffee," Eddie said. A waiter approached. "One double espresso, please," Eddie said. He looked at Maddie. "And for you?"

"Cappuccino, please," Maddie said.

The waiter disappeared into the shop.

Maddie assumed there was some reason for Eddie's actions. Maybe he had arranged to meet his contact here. She looked around. Guess the crook.

It could have been any one of these people – or none of them. That was one thing Maddie had learned from her time in PIC – you couldn't tell the good guys from the bad guys just by looking at them. You had to dig a little deeper than that.

Eddie leaned back in his chair, smiling as he watched people come and go across the busy concourse. "I love stations," he said. "I love places where journeys begin. Stations – airports – sea ports." He looked at her. "The start of a journey is always an adventure, don't you think?" he said. "You never know for sure where you'll be when you get to journey's end."

Maddie looked at him without speaking.

"Take yourself, for instance," Eddie said, leaning towards her across the table. "Did you imagine, when you woke up this morning, that you'd be catching the train to Paris before the day was out?"

"No," Maddie replied. "I don't suppose I did."

The waiter appeared with their drinks. Eddie's eyes were bright as he looked at Maddie. "Life is full of surprises," he said. He lifted his cup. "To trust and friendship," he said.

She picked up her cup. "To honesty," she said. "To the truth."

They both drank.

A silence grew between them.

Confused thoughts thrashed in Maddie's head. Was she right or wrong to be doing this? She wished she could ask someone for advice. Her father. Alex. Danny. Tara. Her gran...

Her mother.

She knew what they would all say: *Get out of there, Maddie. Get away from him – now!*

But she couldn't. It was too late to just cut and run.

There's a bond between us, Maddie.

Eddie was right. Something was keeping them together, but whether it was for good or evil, only time would tell. But Maddie knew one thing – the only way to get closure on her relationship with Eddie Stone was to follow this madness through to the end.

Eddie placed some coins on the table. He stood up. "Shall we go?" he said.

She followed him away from the café.

He headed for the International Terminal.

They were halfway across the concourse before

Maddie realised that Eddie was now carrying a small black leather briefcase. He must have picked it up at the table.

She looked over her shoulder – wondering who had handed it to him, how it had been planted there for him. She had been watching out for just such a thing to happen – and she'd completely missed it.

She looked at him. "That was pretty slick," she said. "What's in the case?"

He smiled. "Two tickets to Paris," he said.

They came to the stairs that led down to the terminal. Eddie paused. He opened the case. Maddie saw a flat white envelope. She also saw a large padded envelope, its sides rounded out by whatever it contained.

Eddie took out the white envelope and snapped the case shut again.

He drew two tickets out of the envelope and examined them.

"Departure time eighteen thirty-nine," he said.

Maddie looked at her watch. It was quarter past six.

She had twenty-three minutes to change her mind.

✪

Eddie's contact had booked them two "Premium" tickets – the most expensive and exclusive seats on the train. They checked in at a special desk and were shown to a private lounge. There were shops, cafés and other amenities. Announcements rang out from time to time, alternating between French and English. Uniformed staff glided about unobtrusively.

As they sat in the half-empty lounge, Maddie watched the minutes tick slowly away.

At 18:20 their train was announced. Eddie stood up. Maddie's eyes were still fixed on the clock. She didn't move. He held a hand out towards her.

She tore her eyes away from the clock and looked at him.

She had finally realised why it had been so difficult for her to make her mind up. It was because, somewhere deep inside, she had the feeling that once she got on that train with Eddie – whatever happened between them – her life would never be the same again.

She ignored his hand. She stood up.

She looked into his face – all doubts gone. "Let's go," she said.

She led the way to the escalator. She stood in front of him as they were conveyed up to the platform. The long, sleek train was waiting for them.

They found their carriage and got on board. A

steward welcomed them and showed them to their seats. The seats were in blocks of four – two pairs facing each other across a table. Maddie sat in the outer seat, facing the engine.

Eddie sat opposite her. He placed the briefcase on the seat next to him.

There seemed to be few other people in their carriage.

Eddie rested his head back against the seat. He was smiling. Maddie held his eyes in a steady, candid gaze. She wasn't confused any more. She felt strangely calm. She was going to do this – and she was going to do it right.

Eddie leaned fowards, his elbows on the table, his hands spread open towards her. "Well, Maddie," he said. "It's a three-hour journey to Paris. What shall we talk about?"

Chapter Twenty-four

The grill pan was stone cold.

The four slices of bacon wallowed in congealed fat.

Chas Lennox came into the kitchen. He peeled his jacket off and threw it over a chair. He headed towards the grill and looked at the unappetising contents of the pan. He tipped the whole mess into the bin, then he opened the fridge door and took out a can of lager. He cracked it open and lifted it to his lips.

A figure stepped silently into the doorway. It approached Lennox from behind – as silent and deadly as a hunting cat.

Before Chas Lennox had the chance to take a single swig from the can, he found himself caught in an armlock. A hand reached over his shoulder and plucked the can from his fingers.

"Hello, Chas," said Alex. "You're nicked."

○

Lennox sat sullenly at the kitchen table, nursing his aching arm. He ached in other places, too. He'd made a big mistake. He'd tried to fight Alex. Bad move. The fight had lasted for twenty-two seconds. Lennox had ended up on the floor – locked down – gasping for breath – promising to behave.

Alex sat on the worktop by the hob. He had already phoned for backup and was waiting for the black van to arrive. He was watching Lennox closely – alert for any tricky moves. The guy wasn't strong or fit enough to outfight him, but he was street-smart. Alex knew better than to underestimate him.

Lennox gave Alex a sideways look. Cunning. Figuring the angles.

"I know what you want," he said, his voice low and sly.

"Do you?" said Alex. "Who's a clever boy, then."

"You want Eddie," Lennox said. "I'll cut you a deal. I give you Eddie and you let me walk out of here. What do you say?"

This was unexpected. What did Lennox know about

Eddie? Alex decided to play along.

"Keep talking," he prompted.

Lennox's eyes narrowed. "He called me earlier this afternoon," he said. "He had a little job for me to do." He licked his lips. "Would you like to know what the job was?"

"I'm listening," Alex said.

"Eddie wanted two train tickets from Waterloo to Paris," Lennox said. "I got them for him. He's going to be on the eighteen thirty-nine train." His eyes glittered like broken glass. "Does that get me out of here?"

"Don't rush me, Chas," Alex said. "I need to make a call." He took out his mobile. He speed-dialled Danny's number.

Danny picked up after two rings.

"It's Alex. I'm with Lennox. He's just told me that Eddie Stone will be on the eighteen thirty-nine to Paris from Waterloo. He's got two tickets, so he's travelling with someone."

Danny's response was rapid and urgent. "He's with Maddie, Alex."

"What?" Alex felt a stab of concern. "How did that happen?"

"It's a long story."

"Tell me later," said Alex. "Go get her back, Danny."
He cut the line.

"So? What happens now?" Lennox asked.

"We wait for the van," Alex answered.

Lennox's face became ugly. "I've given you Eddie. Cut me some slack!"

"I didn't come here about Eddie," Alex said. "I came here to pick you up for questioning in connection with the shooting of the Cooper family last summer."

Lennox made a wild dive for the door.

Alex was on him in three paces. He drove Lennox to the floor. On his face. He sat astride him. He drew a pair of handcuffs out of an inner pocket of his leather jacket. He pulled Lennox's arms around behind him and snapped the cuffs on.

Alex began the official arrest litany. "Charles Lennox, I am arresting you in connection with the death of Eloise Cooper, and for the serious assault on Jack and Madeleine Cooper. You do not have to say anything, but it may harm your defence if you do not mention when questioned something which you later rely on in court. Anything you do say may be given in evidence."

At the end of a long, frustrating day, Alex was finally getting some job satisfaction.

✪

Southampton Row, WC1.

18:15.

The drive to the station was a frantic race against time. And, for Tara, a precarious balance between caution and speed. She couldn't just open up the throttle and go for it. There was too much traffic between Euston and Waterloo. Too many obstacles. She was prepared to risk her own life to rescue Maddie, but she wasn't going to put anyone else in danger.

The car had no siren. She cleared the way by ramming her hand down on the horn. Most cars got the message and moved out of her path. When that didn't happen, Tara got Danny to sound the horn while she spun the wheel to take the car forward.

"Make a call to the station, Danny," Tara said as they sped along. "Tell them to hold the train till we get there."

Danny found the number through the Internet. He dialled.

"Oh, great!" he hissed. "That's just perfect!" He held the phone to Tara's ear. It was the engaged signal.

"Keep trying," Tara said.

She negotiated the loop of the Aldwych and into Lancaster Place. Waterloo Bridge was right ahead. The station was on the south side of the river. They were almost there.

Waterloo Station.

18:33.

They abandoned the car in York Road. There was no time for fancy parking.

They bounded up the steps to the station concourse. Tara was just ahead of Danny as they broke through into the building.

They ran. The concourse was full of people. There was no time for finesse – no time to apologise. Tara went through the startled people like a scythe. Danny was right behind her.

They came to the cool glass-and-steel terminal at the western end of the station. Tara vaulted down the stairs. People were staring.

She jumped the check-in barrier. There were shouts. She ignored them.

Danny was confronted by security guards. He flipped them his PIC ID card. They recognised its authority immediately.

"The eighteen thirty-nine," he panted. "Where?"

One of the guards pointed. "That way. But you're too late. The train is leaving." But Danny was gone.

Tara and Danny bounded up the escalator.

They came to the platform.

A whistle was blowing.

Tara let out a scream of frustration. "No!" The train was gliding slowly away. "*No!*"

Danny threw himself forwards. He hammered his hands on the sealed door of the last carriage. A futile gesture. He tripped and fell flat on the platform.

Tara hauled him to his feet.

They stood together on the platform: panting, winded, defeated. The long train glided smoothly away from them.

Their mad race across London had failed.

❂

"I had nothing to do with the shooting." Chas Lennox was back in the kitchen chair, but this time his wrists were secured at his back by Alex's handcuffs. "I don't know anything about it."

"Whatever you say, Chas." Alex stood at the window. He was watching Lennox closely, but every now and then his fingers would part the blind and he would look down into the street. The black PIC van should be there any time now. Alex was anxious to hand Lennox over to his colleagues and to get on Maddie's trail. He still had no idea how she had got herself hooked up with Eddie Stone. Something must have gone completely haywire with Operation Snake Pit.

It was beginning to look as if everything they tried with Mickey Stone went wrong somehow. Alex hadn't forgotten that the last time Maddie had met up with Eddie, she had almost been killed. That thought did nothing to settle his nerves.

"Listen to me," Lennox pleaded desperately. "I don't know who did the job, but I can tell you who ordered the shooting."

Alex shook his head. "That's old news, Chas," he said. "We already know who masterminded the hit. It was Mickey Stone."

A slow, cunning smile spread across Lennox's face. "Is that what you think?" he said.

Alex stared at him. "Do you know better?"

Lennox nodded. "It was Eddie," he said. "Mickey had nothing to do with it. He didn't even know it was going to happen, till he heard about it on the TV. Eddie set the whole thing up."

Alex couldn't prevent a look of alarm from flickering across his face. Lennox laughed. Alex reached for his mobile.

"If you're planning on trying to arrest him," Lennox continued, his voice sly and oily, "I should warn you – he's got a gun." He winked at Alex. "Don't mess with Eddie Stone – he's not normal. He plays by his own rules." His eyes gleamed. "Eddie seems like a normal bloke on the surface – but underneath he's a total psycho."

Chapter Twenty•five

Waterloo Station.

The International Terminal.

18:40.

"Are you OK?" Tara asked.

Danny nodded, shaky from his tumble on the platform. "I'll live." He dusted himself down, bruised but unhurt. "I guess we blew it."

The guards from the security point were heading towards them.

"We need to talk to someone in authority," Tara said. "We have to get that train stopped."

Danny's mobile chimed.

He flipped it open. A voice spoke.

"It's Alex. Listen very carefully, Danny. We've got problems."

✘

The Golf GTi sped along the M20.

The drive through Southeast London had been a nightmare of delays, but now they were out on the motorway, Tara could really open up. She hadn't spoken for some time. Her mouth was a grim line and her eyes were steely. She was focused on the road ahead, driving hard and fast, controlling the car with extraordinary skill and with absolute concentration.

Danny was watching the SatNav screen. Ashford was still forty-seven kilometres away.

Alex's news had scared them. Maddie was on a train to Paris with the man who had ordered the shooting of her mother and father. And he had a gun.

She was in far worse danger than they had imagined.

They had to make their decision fast.

Stop the train?

No. That was too risky. Eddie Stone would be living on his nerve ends. He would be paranoid. If anything out of the ordinary happened, he might react badly. If the train stopped or even slowed down significantly, he would probably feel threatened. And that wouldn't be good for Maddie.

Eddie Stone had to think everything was under control right up until the very second that he was apprehended. That was the only way to ensure Maddie would come out of this alive.

And the only way to take Eddie out, was to get someone on the train.

The first opportunity to do that would be at Ashford.

The train was due to arrive at Ashford International Station at 19:29.

Danny looked at his watch. It was already 19:07. They had twenty-two minutes to get there.

He glanced at the speedometer.

The way Tara was driving, they might still make it.

✪

The Paris Express.

Maddie's dinner plate lay untouched on the table in front of her. Her stomach was a tight knot. Eating was the last thing on her mind. But Eddie seemed to be enjoying the food.

A complementary four-course meal served on bone china. With a bottle of vintage wine.

A wry thought crossed Maddie's mind: Eddie was certainly escaping the country in style – wined and dined while being whisked towards the English Channel and beyond – into France and all the way to Paris.

And then what?

Good question.

And then Maddie would know for certain whether she was crazy to trust Eddie Stone.

She found him looking at her.

"You should try this wine," he said.

"No. Thank you."

Eddie frowned. "You're not really enjoying the journey, are you?" he said gently. "What are you thinking about, Maddie?"

"I'm thinking that you're a very dangerous man, Eddie," she replied.

He laughed. "I'm as gentle as a lamb," he said. He waved his fork at her, his manner strangely light-hearted. "I saw Brendan Flynn trussed up in the cellar back at the hotel," he said. "You did that to him, didn't you? I'd say you were the dangerous one, here, Maddie." His eyes gleamed. "I wouldn't want to get on your bad side."

"I had no choice about that," Maddie said curtly.

"And I had no choice but to work for my father," Eddie responded. "But I don't work for him anymore. I've finished with all of that." He smiled. "I'm one of the good guys now, Maddie."

She frowned. "I saw you with those men at the

211

hotel," she said. "You were loving every minute of it."

"I was faking it, Maddie," he said earnestly. "You think I should have told them about my plans to make Stonecor legitimate? I wouldn't have lasted five minutes. I was acting."

"You're a very convincing actor, Eddie."

He nodded. "Thank you."

She stared at him. "That wasn't meant as a compliment."

An announcement sounded.

"We will shortly be arriving at Ashford International Station. Customers are reminded that this stop is for boarding only. We are on schedule, and are due to arrive at Paris Gare Du Nord at twenty-two twenty-three, local time."

Maddie looked out of the window. They were coming into a built-up area.

Ashford Station lay dead ahead.

✪

Ashford.

19:27.

Coming off the motorway had slowed Tara down again. There were only so many risks she could take. One too many tricky manoeuvres could result in disaster.

Danny was staring through the windscreen – watching for road signs – shouting instructions. He had phoned ahead to speak to the duty manager at Ashford Station, making sure that they would get instant security clearance to board the train. The duty manager had asked whether they wanted him to hold the train. Danny said no – don't do anything out of the ordinary. It was vital to keep everything as normal as possible.

Danny's eyes kept returning to his watch.

It was taking too long.

It was already 19:29.

Tara cruised round a corner.

The station was in front of them.

Danny let out a whoop.

His relief didn't last long.

A car came nosing out from the left. Tara spun the wheel, swearing under her breath as she fought to keep control.

Their car mounted the pavement. Tara slammed on the brakes. The seat belt bit into Danny's shoulder as he was thrown forwards.

There was a hollow metallic bang as the car hit a concrete bollard and was thrown back.

Danny gasped for breath. Tara was panting with the

shock, her eyes wide, her hands clamped to the steering wheel.

In one rapid move, Danny disengaged his seat belt and threw the car door open. There was no time to lose now. He almost tripped. He stumbled forwards. He regained his balance. He ran.

Tara tasted blood. She had bitten her lip. She tried to open her door, but it was blocked by another bollard.

She wiped the blood off her chin. She struggled to get out of the car through the passenger side. She could see Danny sprinting towards the station.

He disappeared into the building.

The time was 19:31.

❁

The Paris Express.

19:40.

Eddie had pushed his plate aside. He was leaning towards Maddie, his elbows on the table, his hands spread out towards her.

She was sitting right back in her seat, gazing at him, listening to his sad, compelling voice.

He was telling her about his mother's long illness. About the last few weeks of her life. About how thin she became. About her bravery. About her last day.

Maddie's throat was constricted. Her voice was only a whisper. "Why are you telling me this?" she asked.

"So you'll believe me when I tell you that I understand how you feel about losing your mother," he said. "It was a terrible thing to happen. My father may not have pulled the trigger, but he was responsible for her death. He gave the order. I hate him for that. I hate him for ruining your life."

She struggled against a rising flood of emotion. Part of her wanted to scream and rage and strike out at him – part of her wanted to give in, to pull down the barriers between them. To believe him. To trust him completely.

His hands moved closer across the table. "You're a wonderful, extraordinary girl, Maddie," he said. "And you have so much courage."

Maddie's hands were clenched in her lap, fingers locked in a bloodless war.

A silent tear ran down her face.

"My mother is dead," she whispered. "I don't feel very courageous right now."

"Then let me help you," he murmured, his hands stretching towards her. "I'll never let you down, Maddie. You know that, don't you?"

She loosened her hands. She took a long, shuddering breath. She reached out towards him.

It was over.

He had won.

He took her hands in his and rose from his seat, leaning towards her over the table.

She lifted her face, looking into his eyes.

Their heads moved closer.

"Very eloquent, Eddie." The voice was a harsh growl. "You always were a good liar."

Maddie stared at the man who was suddenly standing over them. It was Mickey Stone.

She jerked her hands away from Eddie's. He had fallen back into his seat. He was staring up at his father. His face was drained of colour.

Mickey Stone smiled coldly at him. "Are you surprised to see me, Eddie?" he said. "Did you forget Chas works for me?" He brought his hand down on Eddie's shoulder, pushing him into the window seat. He sat down, his eyes fixed on his son.

"Chas called to tell me about your little trip to Paris," he said. "He's very loyal, Eddie. Unlike some people." He turned to look at Maddie. She was staring at him in silent horror – too stunned to think. "You shouldn't believe the things my son tells you, Miss Cooper," he said. "I had nothing to do with the death of your mother."

"You're lying," Maddie whispered. "Lennox did it – and you just admitted that Lennox works for you."

Mickey Stone smiled grimly. "Chas did do one job for Eddie," he said. "Without my permission, and without my knowledge." He leaned towards her across the table. "Listen very carefully to me, Miss Cooper, because I'm telling you the truth. It was my son who ordered Chas Lennox to kill your father."

"He's lying to you, Maddie," Eddie said. "Don't believe him. You have to trust me."

"I'm not lying," Mickey Stone said. "I would never have given Chas Lennox a job like that. He wasn't up to it." His eyes became deadly. "If I had wanted your father dead, Miss Cooper, I'd have hired a professional hit man." His voice lowered to offer a blood-chilling promise. "If I had given the order, your father would be dead right now and your mother would still be alive. Think about it."

Maddie stared at Eddie. She felt like the world was going crazy around her.

She opened her mouth, hardly able to speak. "Was it you?" she whispered.

She was vaguely aware that Eddie was doing something under cover of the table. Something with his hands. Something with the briefcase.

217

"Why won't you trust me, Maddie?" Eddie's voice was a thin whisper. "I don't understand it. I trust you."

His hand was inside the briefcase, his fingers groping into the padded envelope.

Maddie's mind was reeling.

"You had us shot..." she gasped. "It was you."

Eddie's hand came out of the briefcase. He was holding a gun. Holding it low. Angling his wrist so that the muzzle was aimed part of the time at her and part of the time at his father.

Maddie looked into his eyes. They had gone cold.

"I thought you were different, Maddie," he whispered, his voice soft and chilling. "I thought you were someone special. But you're not. You're just like everyone else. Treacherous and deceitful, worthless and destructive. I was stupid to think I could trust you. I can't trust you at all. You don't deserve to be trusted."

Maddie felt sick. It wasn't just the gun that was terrifying her, it was the tone in Eddie's voice. He didn't sound like the same person any more – he didn't sound sane.

Eddie's eyes turned to his father. "You've ruined everything," he whispered, his voice filling with madness. "Why did you have to come here?"

Mickey Stone's voice was low and calm. "I know why

you're going to Paris, Eddie," he said. "I wouldn't let you run the business, so you were going to destroy it, and me along with it." He shook his head. "I can't let you do that."

Eddie's eyes glittered. His face was distorted by a mad smile. "And how are you going to stop me?" The gun was now aimed firmly at his father.

A sudden movement caught Maddie's eye.

As though in a dream, she watched as Danny's head and shoulders appeared above the back of Eddie's seat. His arm reached down. He had an empty bottle in his hand. He touched the open end against the back of Eddie's neck.

"Don't move, Eddie," Danny said sharply. "I'll shoot you if I have to."

Eddie's body went rigid. His eyes were on Maddie's face. Glazed. Unseeing.

Danny was faking it. He was taking a terrible risk, but it seemed to be working.

"Put the gun down, Eddie," Danny said. "Nice and slow. We don't want any accidents."

But it wasn't going to be that easy.

With a movement as quick as a striking snake, Eddie's arm punched out across the table. The gun was in his fist. He was holding it sideways. His finger was on the trigger. The muzzle was pointing at Maddie's forehead.

"Shoot me and she goes too," he said.

Maddie stared into the ice-blue eyes. The expression in them was deadly – inhuman. She knew at that moment that he would kill her.

"Give it up, son," Mickey Stone said softly. "It's over."

Maddie was half aware of a kind of breathless stillness in the carriage. The other passengers had realised that something bad was happening. So far, shock and fear had kept them back, but the tension couldn't last.

Something had to break.

Something did.

A single drop of liquid gathered at the mouth of the bottle Danny was holding. Eddie felt the wetness against his skin.

The truth hit him like a bolt of lightning. That was no gun at his neck.

His free hand moved with startling speed. He wrenched the bottle out of Danny's fingers.

At the same moment, Mickey Stone threw himself towards his son. His hands dragged Eddie's gun arm down.

Maddie flung herself out of her seat – out of the line of fire.

As she fell to the floor of the carriage, she heard the terrifyingly loud noise of a single gunshot reverberate through the carriage.

There were screams. Shouts of fear and panic.

She heard a sharp cry. A groan of agony.

Someone had been hit.

Chapter Twenty•six

Screaming.

Shouting.

The panicked sounds of people trying to get away from the madman with the gun.

The never-ending rumble of the steel train-wheels on the rail track.

The echoes of that single gunshot.

Fear for her life – terror of Eddie Stone.

All these things filled Maddie's head as she sprawled on the floor of the carriage.

She struggled to get to her feet in the confined space between the seats.

Someone had been shot.

But who?

Danny had leaped on to the train just as the doors were closing. As it had moved off, he had seen Tara come running on to the platform. Too late.

That wasn't good. Tara was a martial arts black belt. Danny hadn't even won his yellow belt yet. The plan they had worked out between them was that Danny would create a diversion and then Tara would go in for the kill.

Danny was on his own now.

He had found the train manager and explained the situation. He had borrowed a steward's jacket. He had made his way to the carriage where Maddie and Eddie Stone were sitting. He had seen Mickey Stone, huddled behind a newspaper in a corner seat at the end of the carriage.

That had been a nasty surprise. What was Mickey Stone doing there?

More than ever, Danny had wished that Tara was with him. What could he do on his own against two generations of the Stone family?

He had kept his head down. Watching and waiting.

A little while later, Mickey Stone had moved from his seat. Danny had followed at a discreet distance. Thinking on his feet.

223

He had seen the gun in Eddie's hand.

Bad news.

He had spotted an empty beer bottle on a table.

Improvise. Keep things moving. Take the initiative.

He had picked up the bottle and had crawled on to the seat behind Eddie. He had lifted himself over the back of the seat. He had seen Maddie's eyes on him.

He had made his play.

For a second or two, Danny had thought he had it all under control.

And then that single drop of beer had betrayed him.

Eddie had been too quick. He had turned the gun on Maddie.

The bottle was snatched out of his hand. He saw Mickey Stone lunge forwards, pulling Eddie's gun arm away from Maddie. He saw Maddie throw herself sideways. He reached over the seat, trying to intervene. He got Eddie's elbow in his face. It knocked him backwards – his whole head was one big ball of pain.

He heard the shot ring out.

He heard the cry.

Someone had been hit.

✖

Maddie used the table to lever herself up. She saw in an instant what had happened.

Mickey Stone had collapsed in his seat, his face tight with pain – his hand pressed to his upper chest. Blood oozed between his fingers. A moment later, he fell sideways off the seat and slumped to the floor.

Maddie looked up at Eddie. He was shaking – staring down at his father – the gun loose in his hand. His face was a mask of disbelieving shock.

"Eddie?" His wild eyes turned towards her. She reached out towards him. "Give me the gun, Eddie."

He stared at her for the space of two or three pounding heartbeats. There was pure horror in his eyes. She would never forget it.

He turned away from her. He gripped the gun tightly. He swung his arm towards the window. He jerked his finger back on the trigger.

The gun fired – blotting out every other sound.

The window shattered. Shards of glass exploded in all directions. There was a hurricane scream of wind through the broken window. Fragments of glass hurtled around the carriage like shrapnel.

Maddie threw her hands over her face. She felt glass splinters cascading over her. The wind roared in her ears.

She lifted her head. She saw Eddie at the window, his hair and clothes torn by the slipstream of the

225

speeding train. For a split second he hung there, his knee on the table, his hand on the window frame. He looked back at her.

"Eddie! No!"

Maddie hurled herself across the table – her hands snatching at him.

He flung himself forwards.

He was gone in a rushing, howling instant.

She was too late.

She hung from the window, blinded by the wind – her face whipped by her own hair. She felt herself being grabbed from behind. She was pulled back into the carriage. She looked over her shoulder. Danny had hold of her.

She heard screaming. "Eddie! No!"

It was her own voice.

✪

Kent.

Ordnance Survey Grid Reference: TR055385.

Two kilometres southeast of Mersham.

Trackside on the London–Paris line.

21:01.

The train stood silent and deserted against a brooding, red sunset. All the passengers were gone, taken back to Ashford in coaches.

There were a number of cars nearby. There were two ambulances.

A PIC forensic team was in the carriage from which Eddie had jumped. Gathering physical evidence. Not that there was much doubt about what had happened. The broken window told its own story.

And there were the eye-witness accounts of two PIC agents: Maddie Cooper and Danny Bell. They had seen the whole thing. The madness. The gun. The struggle. The shooting. The suicidal leap from the train. The full nightmare.

Eddie Stone's body had been found several hundred metres back along the track. He must have died instantly.

His body lay under a blanket on an ambulance trolley. It couldn't be moved until the coroner had done her job. She was on her way.

The gun still hadn't been found.

Agents were scouring the ground alongside the track.

It was just a matter of time.

✪

Maddie couldn't even bring herself to look at the dark shape on the trolley. Alex and Danny were with her. The three of them sat together under the shadow of the

227

train. Maddie felt drained. Hollow. Aching from the inside out. Shattered.

Alex touched her shoulder. She looked up as a paramedic pushed the trolley towards a waiting ambulance.

Another ambulance had already left the scene.

The patient inside the ambulance had been a heavy-set man in his fifties. He'd had close-cropped, iron-grey hair. He'd had a bulldog face – pale and sweaty. A mask had fed oxygen to him. He'd had a bullet in his shoulder. It wasn't a life-threatening injury. Mickey Stone would survive to stand trial. Two armed PIC agents had left in the ambulance with him. Another alongside the driver.

Jack Cooper wasn't taking any chances.

Maddie, Alex and Danny had watched as the ambulance departed.

Danny had promised, "This time, he doesn't get to escape."

☮

Jack Cooper wheeled himself over to the stretcher trolley. He stared at the dark blanket. His face was expressionless, but his knuckles where white as he gripped the arms of his chair.

After a few moments, he reached out a hand and

lifted up the corner of the blanket. He looked at Eddie Stone's face for a few, long seconds.

He spoke in a whisper. "Goodnight, Mr Stone."

He dropped the blanket back over the face. He sat still for a few moments, gathering his thoughts. Then he wheeled himself over to where Tara was busy coordinating the search for the missing gun.

✪

Alex's mobile phone sounded, breaking the weary silence that had grown between the three trainee agents.

He took it from his jacket pocket.

"Yes. Go ahead."

Maddie saw his eyes begin to gleam as the message came through.

"Good work," he said. "I'll tell everyone here." He closed his phone.

Maddie and Danny were both looking at him.

"That was Jackie from Control," he said. "A gun has been found at Lennox's place. Hidden under the floor." He looked at Maddie. "It's the same make and calibre as the one that killed your mother. But that's not the best of it. As soon as Lennox was told they'd got the gun, he spilled his guts. You were right, Maddie. It *was* his voice you heard. He's confessed to the shooting. He's admitted that he was Eddie Stone's hit man."

Maddie let out a gasp of breath. She felt as though a crippling weight had been lifted from her shoulders. It was true. Eddie had ordered the hit. Lennox was the gunman.

She stood up. Her legs felt weak. Her head swam. She walked down towards the huddle of PIC vehicles. She stopped. She turned and stared into the blood-red sky.

The sun was almost on the horizon.

She felt cold. Terribly lonely. Scared.

Alex and Danny approached her, their faces anxious.

"It's all over," Alex said. Maddie understood what he meant. This wasn't just the end of the PIC operation – it was the end of a year in limbo for her and her father. Eloise Cooper's killer had finally been tracked down. Justice could now run its course.

Maddie looked at him. "No," she said quietly. "It isn't over at all. It's never going to be over." She turned and looked at last towards the covered body. "It doesn't change anything."

"You're not alone, Maddie," Danny said.

"I know," she said with a faint smile.

She looked over her shoulder to where her father was sitting.

She walked down towards him. He heard her approach. He turned and looked up at her.

She took his hand and knelt down at his side.

She had no sense of fulfilment. No sense of completion.

"I nearly trusted him, Dad," she whispered. "I was beginning to believe everything he said. How could I have been so stupid?"

"You're not stupid, Maddie. Look at me." She gazed up into her father's face. "Today, you did the most important thing a PIC agent can ever do," he said. "You came out alive. I'm very proud of you, Maddie."

She smiled sadly, resting her head against his knee.

"I miss Mum so much," she said.

Her father rested his hand on her head. "I know," he said. "So do I."

The sun went down like a ball of blood.

Night came flooding in.

The day ended like the slamming of a huge door.

And the nightmare was over.

SPECIAL AGENTS
DEEP END

Your life can change in a second

Maddie Cooper's life changed in just one second.
She and her parents were gunned down in the
street by an unknown assailant. Maddie's mother
was killed and her father left in a wheelchair.
Maddie signs up as a trainee in her father's notorious
flying squad: Police Investigation Command.

She teams up with Alex Cox, ace undercover man,
and Danny Bell, an electronics' whizz-kid with a
razor sharp mind.

Alex, Danny and Maddie – three teenagers fighting
crime on the streets of London.

0-00-714842-9

HarperCollins *Children's Books*

SPECIAL AGENTS
FINAL SHOT

A death threat hangs over Britain's tennis ace

It's a week before the Wimbledon Tennis
Championships and all eyes are on British hopeful,
Will Anderson. But when a murder investigation
leads police to a stash of mutilated photographs
of Will, it becomes horribly clear that he is
the murderer's next victim.

When police Investigation Squad trainees, Alex,
Danny and Maddie go undercover with Will,
things turn nasty.

Alex, Danny and Maddie – three teenagers fighting
crime on the streets of London.

0-00-714844-5

HarperCollins *Children's Books*

SPECIAL AGENTS
COUNTDOWN

A bomb has been set to go off in Central London, and time is running out...

Police Investigation squad trainees, Alex and Danny, are on a tough assignment. They are acting as bodyguards for a powerful Italian businessman and his ambitious girlfriend. Alex and Danny are convinced that Prima's life is in danger, but he seems reluctant to accept their help.

Across the capital, hot-dog and ice-cream vans are being systematically attacked – Maddie is involved in the strange case of the Ice-Cream Wars. When the two cases collide, Danny, Alex and Maddie are in serious danger.

Alex, Danny and Maddie – three teenagers fighting crime on the streets of London.

0-00-714843-7

HarperCollins *Children's Books*